I0625132

SUMMARY

Book II in the Knights of the Board Room series

On a cycling trip to the Berkshires, CFO Lucas Adler stumbles on a woman pleasuring herself in a glade on her Harley. When she slips through his fingers without leaving her name, he's haunted by her taste, her scent...the sadness in her eyes. Then she walks into his board room.

This time, he'll prove he can be her champion, no matter what life throws at her.

i

CONTROLLED RESPONSE

A Knights of the Board Room Novella

JOEY W. HILL

Controlled Response

A Knights of the Board Room Novella - Book #2

Copyright © 2019 Joey W. Hill

ALL RIGHTS RESERVED

Cover design by W. Scott Hill

SWP Digital & Print Edition publication January 2019 by Story Witch Press, 452 Mattamushkeet Dr., Little River, South Carolina 29566, USA

Berkley Digital & Print Edition publication February 2008 by the Penguin Group, 375 Hudson Street, New York, New York 10014, USA

The following material contains graphic sexual content meant for mature readers. Reader discretion is advised.

Digital ISBN: 978-1-942122-84-5

Print ISBN: 978-1-942122-88-3

CHAPTER ONE

*F*orty-five miles. God, the only thing better than this was sex. Sex done exceptionally well. As Lucas crested the hill, pushing the burn in his legs, he snagged his water bottle to take a measured draught. Releasing the bike handlebars to coast hands-free, he shifted his hips to negotiate the inevitable curve. No such thing as a straight line or a flat expanse this deep in the Berkshires. Every downward slope followed by a challenging upward one. Like the curves of a woman's body. Or her mind.

Ben had given him shit about hopping a charter here for the weekend when they were still figuring out how to make the numbers work for the Mancuso plant operation. But it was all bullshit, because Ben knew Lucas did his best problem solving while cycling, just as the legal advisor did it by finding the prettiest ass available and immersing himself in it. When they came back to the office Monday, Ben would fix the legal snarls, and Lucas would crunch the numbers into manageable pieces. Hell, Matt should save the money on their corner offices. Though Lucas had to admit he liked his Baton Rouge city view, with the backdrop of the Mississippi River.

It was time for a lunch break and a stretch, if he could find the spot his buddy Marcus had told him was right off the road around here. He was pretty deep in the Berkshire farm area, but tourists did have a way of finding the hot spots. Still, Marcus had stressed "hid-

1

den," even giving him GPS coordinates for the exact location, give or take ten feet.

There it was. As he rolled across the shoulder, he saw the narrow deer trail. A couple broken twigs and some spoor suggested the brown-eyed creatures had passed through recently.

It was a short hike, so it worked as a good cool-down. The light racing bike was easy to carry, even with his gear. Marcus had said the glade would have a stream, soft grass for a nap, and a frame of trees for the sky that would make Lucas think he'd fallen into a nest made by Heaven itself. Marcus was a gallery owner, brushing shoulders with New York art types, so such metaphors were to be expected. Or maybe the description had come from Thomas, his spouse, or life partner, whatever they called it. It sounded like a good place and Lucas wouldn't dwell on what they might have done there.

To each his own, but his preference definitely ran to heart-shaped asses of a different gender. Skin like cream, and tender pink lips hidden like treasure between not-too-firm, not-too-soft thighs. Just like Goldilocks, he knew when they were just right.

Lately, it had been just okay. Some lovely ladies, intelligent, beautiful, and willing. Business associates on the same time schedules, which discouraged anything deeper on either side, but ensured dinner dates and sexual release were no farther than a cell phone call. He was CFO for Kensington & Associates, after all, so he didn't have trouble with that.

But maybe it was watching Matt, the head of K&A, with his new wife, Savannah, during the past year. The way they'd taken the leap of faith together, and their love just seemed to grow and grow. Not like a molasses flood, drowning everyone in reach in gooeyness. More like the quiet reassurance of the ocean's murmur. Timeless, clean, overwhelming. Proof that there was a greater purpose here. Maybe Lucas was ready for something deeper himself. Maybe that was why he was cycling and Ben was likely hip deep in pussy by now.

As he stepped into the clearing, anticipating the tranquility, he came to a dead stop, his thoughts scattering like a game of 52-card pickup.

Marcus hadn't mentioned the spot came with a half-naked girl on a motorcycle.

Either that, or Lucas had been run over by a minivan and didn't realize he was dead, stumbling into everything Heaven should be. If so, he was profoundly thankful to the minivan driver.

He blinked. Yes, it was definitely a woman, stretched out on the curved seat of a Night Rod series Harley. At one time, she'd apparently been wearing black jeans with riding chaps over them, for they were in a crumpled pile next to the bike, leaving her lower body clad only in a pair of silky ivory panties. Her feet were braced on the handlebars, legs spread, ass snugged down in the driver's seat while her upper body was arched over the hump to the passenger seat. The toned legs and generous ass were taut, for her fingers were tucked into the panties. Thanks to the blessing of filmy material, he could see the individual movements of the digits.

She was wearing a corset. Ivory-colored as well, with one strap falling off her shoulder and elevating her breasts enough they were accentuated by the slightest breath. Just a touch of lace at the low décolletage that tempted full exposure from the crescent stretch of her torso. The corset hooked in front, so would lie flat under the heavy white T-shirt she'd been wearing, also lying in the grass. Tiny earphones for a music player were tucked into ears as delicate as porcelain, half hidden by her hair, skeins of white gold long enough to fall over the top of the rear tire. A few strands were scattered by the breeze across her face, teasing wet, parted lips. Her bare feet flexed against the chrome bars as she apparently hit a good spot, biting her lip. Since her eyes were closed, golden lashes fanning her cheeks, he imagined she was deep in some fantasy, picturing her fingers as someone else's.

Or perhaps she was thinking about someone watching her, getting hungrier for a taste of the pussy she'd teased into a wetness that had soaked the crotch panel. Someone who wanted to slide his hands under her, grip that delectable ass, and tongue her first through the saturated silk. Bite her clit through her panties. Women loved that, the buffer to stimulation that provided friction, helped warm them up, so that when he finally pulled the cloth out of the way and tasted creamed flesh, they would be writhing, begging.

God, he loved eating pussy. Second best thing to fucking it.

A gentleman—not to mention a smart man—would have backed away. But he couldn't make his feet move. This was undeniably a gift from God, and he was a devout Methodist. Okay, at least when he went home to Iowa during Christmas and attended church with his parents. Regardless, there was a higher power, a higher order. Hadn't he just been thinking that? Maybe this was an answer.

Yes, Lucas. In your search for a deeper relationship, God has sent you to a private photo shoot from Penthouse.

Hey, crazier things had happened. Like his spontaneous decision now, to become part of her fantasy. As he moved forward, he hoped she wasn't armed.

Oh, she'd so needed this. Cassandra didn't like being away from home, but she'd had to come to Hartford to close this deal. Two days of managing the negotiation had been bad enough, but she'd had to deal long-distance with crisis after crisis at home, from the minor issues that came up with her younger siblings, to a frantic call from the nanny, saying her black sheep brother had gotten as close as the security gate. Fortunately, the guard had sent him on his way. Everything was now okay there.

But just as she'd been waiting to fly home to Baton Rouge, anticipating being there before bedtime so Nate could sing her a new song he'd learned, she'd received a frantic call from the general manager. The deal she'd just finalized had unraveled, thanks to the key players having an unfortunate exchange over post-meeting drinks the night before.

Knitting it back together had involved a trip back to the Hartford office and some corporate diplomacy. Plus some tactical bullying of those same key players, shaming them for having almost dumped a sixty-million-dollar contract over some childish perceived insult.

That detour had kept her in the area an extra day, so when she'd passed the motorcycle dealership and saw that they did day-rentals for enjoying the Berkshire scenery, she'd thought, why the hell not? She'd chosen the Night Rod and headed out with a map.

Finding this glade had been an extraordinary accident. Pulled over to take a break, she'd seen a pair of deer slipping into the forest. She'd brought a camera, wanting to take some pictures for the kids, so when she'd followed their path, heard the inviting rush of water, she found a stream with a small waterfall, a spot too far off the beaten path for

4

anyone to find. Perfect. Even though she was far from home, the idea of being far from anyone, out of the eye of the world completely, was exactly what she needed.

It seemed sometimes that all she dealt with were children. She much preferred her siblings to those well into supposed adulthood. Was every man in the world looking for Mommy? Did any of them know how to use their brains and take charge, hold the reins comfortably? She'd met precious few like that.

As she'd sat in the grass, leaning against the comforting bulk of the bike, she'd closed her eyes, imagined that hard bulk as such a man. Lying back between his legs, the two of them enjoying the quiet beauty of the setting. He would slide his hands up to cup her breasts, tease the nipples with relentless skill as he pushed her hair aside to kiss her throat. He'd hold her fast when her legs moved restlessly in the grass, needing his touch between them, something he held just out of reach to drive her need higher.

In a house of five kids, with her responsibilities as their guardian, there was little privacy, even to do this. Often she felt like a bottle of soda, shaken to the point of near explosion. Jesus, she'd even resorted to adolescent metaphors for her sexual frustration.

She decided she wanted to stretch her body out on the seat of the muscle bike, strip down to nothing but panties and corset, and make herself come. All while imagining herself as the pinup of some virile god's fantasy, watched by him through the trees. As she adjusted herself against the curves of the seat, dropped her head back, she closed her eyes and let the fantasy play out in her mind.

She'd know he was there, so her movements would be provocative, blatantly carnal, until he couldn't resist any longer and came to her. He'd turn her over the back of the bike, bind her wrists to the pedals, spread her legs wide over the rear tire, the sun's heat on the chrome burning her flesh, and oh, God, she'd be dripping for his cock. But instead he'd kneel first, go to work on her with his mouth, until she was screaming, begging.

She put on her ear phones so she wouldn't worry about every rustle made by a woodland creature, the snapping of twigs. No one was out here, and she didn't want to care anyway. Truth to tell, it wasn't a bad fantasy, imagining someone stumbling upon her. Someone whose name she didn't need to know, who wouldn't let her negotiate or get away with anything. Who would see through every ploy and sweep her choices away.

"Please..." She knew she'd spoken her plea aloud, a whisper, though she couldn't hear it over the hard bass line. When her eyes opened on a brief flicker to let in sunlight, they stayed open. Widened.

Apparently, some perverse nature god had answered her silent plea.

~

He was outlined by the mid-afternoon sun, but the shadowing only enhanced everything she wanted to see. Tall, which she liked, because she was five-eight. Golden-blond hair pushed back, highlighted with darkened streaks from sweat. He was shirtless, the muscles glistening as if oiled. She'd seen bodies with swollen and bunched muscle, but he was as compact as a spring. Flat pectorals, one or two faint veins following the curves of his biceps. The small silver medallion he wore, perhaps a religious symbol, fell in the ridged vee that divided the pecs and coaxed the press of her thumbs. There was nothing wasted on him. While the arms were muscular, she could see the architecture of his collarbone and rib cage, the frame it provided for the tight stomach that wasn't a six-pack, just a slab of smooth muscle, with an indentation of navel that looked as firm.

Tanned, he wore nothing but a pair of tight bike shorts and biking cleats showing off a pair of calves and thighs also roped with taut muscle.

He was a young god by anyone's standards, but the shorts and shoes said he was definitely of her species. A man who'd interrupted something embarrassingly personal.

She wasn't the type to jump up shrieking over it. Kind of beside the point now anyway. She was the type to tell someone to fuck off and let her get on with it, and watch him run in terror. But unlike some of the infantile examples of manhood she'd been dealing with the past couple days, he didn't strike her as the bolting kind. It interested her, made her blood ratchet up a few degrees, her body obviously enjoying the view as she weighed what to do next. Or maybe she'd just see what he did next.

While she waited, her gaze lifted to his mouth. The lean, athletic face which matched the body confirmed he didn't play—he competed. He had the long, sloping jaw she imagined an Egyptian prince might have. Lips with a touch of sensual fullness to them, and a short hairstyle, just a scattering of strands feathering his high forehead. A tapering to short sideburns. He had a hairstylist who knew his or her business, which said money, but the body was a hundred percent from the sweat of his brow. She liked the way the silver medallion lay on his bare skin. She wanted to taste the metal chain and the sweat of it beneath, the salt of him.

As he noted her regard, he casually dropped to a squat, his forearms propped on his spread thighs, fingers grazing the earth. Maybe because he could see her earplugs, he didn't speak, but it intensified the moment, encouraging her to continue.

She had a Beretta in the backpack and knew how to use it. She'd also had self-defense courses, enough to know isolating herself was stupid, since the first line of self-defense for a smart woman was not to put herself in dangerous situations. But she doubted many psycho serial rapists went out on their bicycles in the rural Berkshires, seeking chance encounters with lone women.

His attention was on her lips now, her throat, sweeping down over the corset, a question in his eyes, for of course it wasn't most women's choice of practical underwear. But then he moved his gaze back to her hand. She'd frozen at his appearance, but she still had two fingers inside the panties, lying on her quivering clit, the other two fingers on the outside, her thumb in the crease of her thigh.

Keep going. He mouthed it, she was sure. From the look in his steady gray eyes, it wasn't a request.

She stared at him. *Breathe slow. Even. Hold it steady.* The corset required that.

Even an orgasm could get too out of hand, and she had a feeling it was about to, for as his lips formed the words, her clit shuddered under the bare friction of her still fingers.

He was waiting to see if she would continue. She had no idea what that would make her in his eyes, but why should she care? He wanted her to continue, and hell yes, she wanted to continue. She was far from home here.

When she began to move her fingers, his gaze immediately

returned there. Holy God, who knew that actually being watched was ten times more stimulating than fantasizing about it? And it had been a pretty good fantasy at that. Still, she closed her eyes. Reaching over her head, she found the crisscross of black bungee cords holding her pack. When she slid her free hand under them, the cords cut against her skin, goading her imaginings about her god binding her as he spread her this way, while his mouth...

She sought restraint for her pleasure. That alone spiked Lucas's response. With his casual bed partners being primarily business-women who felt they had to hold the upper hand, it wasn't easy to find one who naturally desired the more dominant forms of sex he preferred. He wondered if that was the reason she wore a corset under her clothes.

God in Heaven, what was a woman like this doing in a secluded glade, having to pleasure herself? The way she'd looked at him, that half-challenge, daring him to run or stay, laced with a sensual desperation that said *Don't ruin this*, had added to the intrigue.

Now he rose, moved to her. As he laid a hand on her raised calf, her gaze sprang open. He stayed that way, not retreating, giving her time. As he smelled her arousal, his nostrils flared. Her gaze registered it, her breath quickening. When she made a visible effort to modulate it, he noted she seemed to be using the corset to control the level of her own arousal. Interesting.

He leaned forward, just enough to have her blue eyes widen a fraction. Pausing, he listened to the faint sound of what was coming through her player. "Hot Blooded," by Foreigner. It told him what pace she'd been setting for herself. But if he was the stimulus, rather than Foreigner's bass line, he thought something else might work better.

Since the player was tucked into the open flap of a saddlebag, he drew it out by the cord so she wouldn't think he was rummaging through her things, then scrolled through the menu.

She had eclectic music taste. Ballads, rock, jazz of the smooth variety. But she also had some things that were off the beaten path. Edgy music that could take the mind to a new place, where the unimaginable might become acceptable. He hit the song he wanted.

"Destiny," by Zero 7. Had he played the song because of the title? No, this guy wasn't that cheesy. He'd known the song, knew it had a dark urgency to it. The haunting opening strains talked about a woman alone in her hotel room, watching pay channel porn and dreaming of her lover. There was a loneliness to it. It was about desire, not thought. The need for someone to understand her, down to the dark, below-the-soul levels.

So he knew the song. But how did he know it would be the right song for this moment, for her?

He was still leaning over her, his gray eyes studying her with an intensity that suggested...not invasion, but as if he was figuring her out. When his gaze finally dropped to her mouth, she had to swallow. As his attention continued to descend, he might as well have put his hands on her, because she felt the weight of his touch in his gaze. He smelled of sweat. Basic earth, male strength.

Men fell short in many ways, but they could sometimes be relied upon for this. He'd just happened on the rare moment when his abilities and her needs were in perfect accord. Lucky him. Lucky her. In this clearing, where he didn't know her name, she'd take it, because he'd done all the right things, made all the right moves, the stages of the dance all male animals had to know to win the willingness of a female. Circling, nonthreatening approach, respectful, but knowing when to switch gears and make the request a demand, bring the force of passion to the mix. It was amazing that humans, supposedly the most intelligent of all species, often fumbled the steps even a field mouse could handle.

As his gaze rose, pinned her again, she gave a bare movement of her head. A nod. Yes. God, yes. But she wouldn't help him. She was tired of orchestrating the whole damn world so it would work the way it should. She wanted to see if someone else could do it.

Usually, she felt compelled to direct. *Touch me here, squeeze that. Kiss me more.*

But when sex was like choreographing a major Broadway production, it was too exhausting to be worth the bother, really.

Putting his hands on her waist, he spanned it, his hands over the tight lacing. Then he moved upward, slow, not as if he was doing it to please her, but as if he was learning her for himself, which pleased her more.

Slow, slow, he held her firmly as his strong fingers moved up over her rib cage. This was a man who not only knew how to touch women, but that each one needed to be handled uniquely, an important component of the foreplay.

As he reached her breasts, he stopped, his forefinger and thumb fitting beneath each. She wanted to draw a deeper breath, but couldn't. She had to keep herself calm. Even. She could do that. If she could do it right now, she could do it anytime. She wouldn't touch him. That would help. But Jesus, the body this man had. She wanted to trail her fingers down his sides, feel the prominent ribs that racked into the muscular abdomen, play at the snug band of the cycling shorts which showed the sleek curve of a sizable erection. Hadn't she heard somewhere they didn't wear any underwear under those?

When she made herself look up, she couldn't prevent a groan as he cupped her breasts, squeezing just enough so they swelled farther out the top of the corset. Not gentle. He didn't hurt her, but he conveyed his desire. The dangerous spark in his gaze at her groan told her he could get a lot rougher, if that was the direction the tone went. He didn't mind getting down and dirty as needed to make it blow-your-mind sex.

If she could get all that from one look, she was still fantasizing. But that was okay. For once, she wasn't going to scale back her expectations just because they appeared unrealistic. If he did everything perfectly, she'd know she was dreaming, no harm done. Even if he did a couple things wrong, she still wouldn't be tossing him out anytime soon. Then his hand went to the first hook of the corset.

Freeze fantasy.

Automatically, Cass caught his wrist with her free hand, an unspoken direction. *That needs to stay on.*

The god toyed with it, his fingers shifting beneath her grip. She suspected he could make short, deft work of the undergarment. It was an effort to hold on to her resolve, because she wanted those long fingers, wanted to explore the shape of his knuckles, the lines between them, the broad shape of the palm. One more moment, and she knew she'd give in.

Then he gave her an inclination of his head, a twist of the sensuous lips. Not capitulation. He was just letting her have her way. For now. It stoked the need in her, and pulling her hand away from his flesh didn't ease it. Now one large hand slid back down to her waist. The other closed around her wrist and withdrew the hand she had in her panties. The motion dragged her fingers over her clit, and that, combined with his intent, was like electrical current. Bringing her damp fingers to his mouth, he took them between his lips, sucked them in deep.

A man who took the reins from a woman in a sexual situation, so effectively that it left no doubt who was in charge. That was what she'd wanted, right?

"Ah." Her body undulated on the seat, a sinuous emulation of what it wanted, before she could stop it. Those full lips were firm and soft at once, his mouth hot, teeth nipping, laving fingers covered with her scent. As he drew them out, he lowered her wet hand, as if he was going to place it on his chest.

Too much temptation, the idea of trailing damp fingers over his muscled flesh, marking him. She closed her fingers into a ball, drew it back to herself.

Again he allowed it, watching her closely all the while. The music had changed once again. Back to Foreigner's "Hot Blooded." It sparked a fire in her, such that she raised a leg, intending to place the sole of her foot on his tempting chest and shove him back, force him just to watch her. Instead, in a smooth motion, he closed his hand on her ankle, pushed it up to his shoulder, and then dropped to one knee.

As he hooked her leg in a firm grip she couldn't shake, panic came and went, gone fast, because he put his mouth on her, over the silky fabric of the panties.

"Oh." The music boiled through her, warring with any protests, egging him on.

The bass line was her heartbeat, pounding hard against her chest, the guitar riffs her gasping breath, too much, overwhelming. If he'd stumbled around like most guys did down there, she might have freaked out and shaken him, but she was too aroused, and his mouth knew what to do even better than her way-too-familiar fingers. A scrape of the clit with his teeth, long, dragging licks of his tongue up the filmy fabric, the friction of it galvanizing her hips to his mouth, wanting to feel the press of his nose, the rasp of his cheeks on her thighs. Tomorrow, she wanted to see the marks, wanted it to chafe when she walked. Evidence that she'd had this over-the-top moment with a stranger.

She twisted, he held her still. She bucked, he moved with her. His mouth was relentless, taking her over from the second it was on her. Foreigner was as merciless as he was, moving from "Hot Blooded" to "Urgent." No fucking kidding. She wanted that climax so badly, but she wanted more, too, an uneasy, yearning feeling she couldn't stifle. Her vision was graying. Oh, damn it all, she couldn't breathe.

He knew that, too. Already rising, moving up her body, hands reaching for the corset.

"No. Don't take it off," she gasped. "Don't."

He muttered an oath she could hear even over the music, with his mouth so close to her ear, but he slid his hands under her arms and lifted her so she was leaning into his body, her cheek on the slick chest muscle. His fingers went to the adjustable laces at the back. Yeah, right. Most guys took five minutes fooling with a bra strap. She was an idiot. She'd probably asphyxiate before...

The garment loosened, more than she wanted to admit was needed, but she could breathe. Of course, she was inhaling him at the same time as the oxygen. Sun-warmed flesh, dense muscle. Feeling the touch of his hands on her and oh, holy hell, what was he doing now?

Using one hand to sweep aside her hair, he laid his lips on the bump of vertebrae, just at her nape, still holding her close against his upper body.

The climax swept over her so fast, there was no anticipating it. It ricocheted up from where the ribbed seat pressed against her pussy, still spasming from the memory of his mouth, to her neck, where his lips rested now. He kept a tight grip on her hair, holding her head still beneath that erotic kiss. As she rocked herself against the seat helplessly, he grasped one of her buttocks, squeezing hard to add male demand to her jerking rhythm, working her against the friction of the seat until she was making frenzied cries, pushing against the solid wall of him. God, she wanted him between her legs, instead of a beast of metal. Hammering into her, holding her down.

The thought brought her down quickly, quicker than she wanted. She was shaken. Shaking, still catching her breath. As he'd pulled her up, it had yanked her ear phones free, so now the music was her own rasping breaths, the birds, the rush of water, the wind. The drumming of his heart, his own ragged sounds.

"Little idiot," he murmured, his jaw along her temple. She heard a faint Midwest accent under the blatant edge of desire. "You could have passed out."

"Well, who knew you'd be good at this?"

She said it without thinking and cursed herself. Guys got off on that kind of flattery, took it as invitation for more. She didn't want to stroke his ego, not when he'd ripped her open like that. Forced her to loosen her self-imposed restraints and turn control over to him.

Wrapping his hand in her hair, he canted her head back. Before she could think of something more quelling to say, he shocked her again by slamming his mouth down on hers, taking it over, and everything attached to it. Drinking deep, he made it everything a kiss should be. Fire, mind-altering, wet, demanding, scraping things raw that would scream in the open elements when he took his mouth away, so that she'd beg for it to return.

Raising his head when she was nowhere near sated, he held his grip so she couldn't try to follow his mouth. "I was just getting started, sweetheart."

Since he was still giving her that penetrating look, it suggested he was used to assessing things closely, determining what made them tick. But he disrupted her anxiety over that when he released her hair to run his hand beneath it, caress her nape in a way that said every time he touched her there, he'd remember what had shattered her.

"Now, let me give you a real climax." As his gaze heated, she began to moisten again, anticipating. "If you thought what I did before was good, there've been too many losers in your life who didn't appreciate how they could make you sing."

A backhanded compliment for sure, she told herself, trying to keep the sensual intent of the words from muddling her mind more than he already had. Implying she was sexually deprived if she let something like a couple minutes of lip play get her off.

Bastard.

"What's your name, sweetheart?"

She shook her head and he tipped up her chin, a trace of impatience in his eyes. "I want to know."

"A name comes with expectations."

"Identity," he agreed. "Repeat dates."

She couldn't afford a man like this in her life, for certain. He'd almost made her smile. "I'm taken."

He blinked once. "No, you're not."

Someone more inexperienced would have retorted, "How do you know?" But when words were used as weapons, she could hold the upper hand. She merely met him eye to eye and stayed silent, trying not to think about the fact she was wearing only soaked panties and a way-too-loose corset. While he was wearing a pair of shorts that should be illegal.

"If you were taken," he said, a sexy, rough edge to his voice, his hand tightening on her sensitive neck, "I'd see him, smell him. There'd be a hint of his aftershave on your breasts, where he started the day by suckling your nipples, or razor burn where his jaw scraped your tender flesh. Your lips would be swollen from his kisses." When she tried to turn her head, he dragged his jaw along the side of her neck, then placed his mouth there, spoke against her tingling skin. "Or I'd have smelled him on your cunt. Because if he doesn't mark you as his every morning before you walk out the door, he's insane."

Hadn't she compared this man's initial approach to that of an animal? After a statement like that, he was pure animal for sure, stating possession in terms understood by beasts of the forest. As well as alpha males with a primal code like this, an undercurrent that she knew women sensed but most could never truly understand. Even as they were hopelessly drawn to it.

Still, women had their own code to survive such a devastating assault. Drawing her head back, she managed a cool smile reflected by no other part of her quivering body, but it was a starting point. "I said I'm taken. I didn't mean by a man. I'm taken by the demands of my life, and you're not part of it. Nor am I inviting you. Only into this moment."

"So that's what this is about." He dipped his finger into the crevice between her breasts, tugged at the corset.

"What?"

"You wear it beneath your clothes. It's not fashion. Control is very important to you."

"It's important to everyone."

"A woman in a corset has to be constantly aware of the state of her body," he observed. "Never getting too flustered, stressed. It's an armor of sorts, but a paradoxical one. Because while the parts so tightly laced inside it lose some sensitivity to a man's touch, the parts above and below become far more sensitive because of the constriction. The trail of a finger along the buttock, just below the corset hem. Or the lightest kiss on the pillow of a breast. Or even the nape." His hand passed there again.

When he put his lips back on her shoulder, she had to ball her hands into fists. She wanted to slide her hands down the curve of his bare back to feel the ridges of spine, how low those shorts came on his hips. Find out if she could slip her hands beneath the tight band to explore the design of his lower back, the rise of his tight ass.

"Let me go down on you again, sweetheart. Let go of your precious control. Give me the bliss of eating your sweet pussy and hearing you scream for me."

She closed her eyes. *I really, really want to, which is why I can't.* "I need some water first. Do you have any?"

A pause. Raising his head, he studied her. "I do. I left my bike just over there. But playing the coward doesn't seem to be your style. If you're going to leave, you're the type who'd just knock a man flat on his ass and walk right over him, not look for a running head start."

"And you're the type who wouldn't get out of the way."

"Not if the fight is worth winning."

I can't say no to you. She'd had her twenty minutes, and that was all she could afford. "I'm out of time. I've got to go."

Moving away from his intoxicating proximity, she grabbed up her jeans, pulled them on while he leaned on her bike seat, watched her silently. She tied on the chaps, fingers trying not to fumble beneath his gaze as she performed the intimate task. When she found her T-shirt, she looked down, realizing she needed to tighten the corset laces. Her breasts were in danger of coming out entirely. It was possible she'd even given him a glimpse of her nipples once or twice in her haste.

Well, she'd call it just compensation for taking off on him.

"Allow me." He'd shifted when she'd been pointedly ignoring him, hoping he'd just vanish, and so now he was right behind her. "Stand still."

As she stiffened, uncertain whether to move away or not, his hand snaked around her waist and up, lifting the corset so the underwire was more fitted beneath her breasts. While he almost impersonally ran his hand over the cups, her nipples hardened from the passing heat of his touch. The liquid pooling between her thighs increased. He adjusted the laces, tightening, tightening again, until a breath escaped from her, a hint of a moan to it.

"You like that, don't you? You like it when a man binds you." His voice had lowered, animal urgency to it, his hands starting to slide downward, taking her resolve there as well.

She jerked away, knowing if he pulled her back so she could feel the hard line of his cock, she'd be lost. She'd let him plow her like a field. Yanking on the T-shirt, she turned, found her boots, and yanked them on as well. A quick grab at the handlebars and she had the twist for her hair she'd left there, whipping it up into a tight bun on her neck.

"Transformation. All armor in place now."

She ignored him, pleased when she managed a flippant tone. "The room's yours. If you want to continue."

Though she really didn't want the provocative image of him stripping off his shorts to lie naked in the grass as God made him, his hand pumping what appeared to be an impressively proportioned cock. All muscles straining as he thought of her, as come spewed from him, wetting his thighs, his smooth ball sac, that hard belly where she could lick it off. Sweet Mother Mary.

"Don't cheapen it." He stepped forward, but surprised her when he didn't reach out to touch her. Even so, she felt the need to pick up the helmet, hold it as a casual barrier between them, all while trying to give him a nonchalant look.

Finally, when she thought she couldn't stand his silent scrutiny another moment, he leaned in. His body pushed against the helmet, brought the pressure of it against the churning in her belly. Despite herself, her lips parted, her eyes seeking his. "My mistake was in giving you a choice," he said. "Next time I get you alone, I won't do that. I'll restrain you the way you wanted to be, and then I'll make you come so hard you'll think you've died. You won't run away from me again. And I'll have the truth about why you feel you need to run now."

Unclogging vocal cords glued together by aching lust was not easy, but she managed it. "To the next time then," she said. A taunt, because of course they'd never see one another again. Moving around him, she strode to the bike.

She wished she could let him know how much she wanted to stay. She was sorry that she'd turned it into this. But he'd managed to kick in the door to her darkest needs in less than twenty minutes, and she couldn't afford to get lost there. It was for the best.

No, the best thing was to let him sate them both, spend another volatile hour together, and then go their separate ways as two strangers who'd enjoyed the novelty of an unexpected sexual encounter. Leaving a challenge in the air like this wasn't good. But he was right. She was being a coward, because if she stayed, she might just want to take him home. And she wouldn't embarrass herself, wouldn't reveal she was so desperate for this type of intimacy she would cling to a stranger. That was almost as pathetic as losing her perspective, making this about more than sex, and ruining it for both of them.

Because she wanted to apologize to him for that, she thought instead about clipping him, enough to make him stumble backward. She didn't, but he did something worse to her. As she passed him at a slow idle, her booted feet balancing her, his hand closed on her arm, so she released the handlebar. He didn't do anything to bring her to a halt, just followed the line of her arm down to her elbow, the tender skin of her forearm, and closed briefly on her fingertips before he let her hand pull free.

She could escape him, but not the irony of it. In his grasp, under the tantalizing hint of his control, she'd felt freer than she had in a very long time.

No, she definitely couldn't afford a man like him in her life.

CHAPTER TWO

"*T*urns out they're sending over someone else to help us work out the final contract points this morning," Jon commented, setting his organizer on the conference room table. "Allan contracted the flu. Johnson called over to Pickard Consulting to send one of their people instead."

Lucas swore, slapping his legal pad down. "This is the type of pissing contest Johnson's been doing throughout this whole thing. I'll bet he talked to Pickard a week ago."

"They're sending Cassandra Moira," Jon added.

Ben whistled. "Big guns, that one."

When Peter lifted a brow, he chuckled. "And those aren't bad either, you complete tit addict."

Peter shot him a grin as Ben continued for Lucas's benefit. "She's one of Pickard's best, groomed right out of school. She's known for getting the job done and walking away from the table with more than you wanted to give away, but making you feel damn good about it. Be particularly careful about her, Lucas. She's hell on wheels on details. I think Pickard had her brain replaced with a CPU."

"We should cancel. We don't have to take this shit. Hell, let's make him think we're pulling out. Maybe he'll have a fatal heart attack and we won't have to deal with this crap anymore."

Jon lifted his brows, exchanged a look with Peter, but it was Ben who stated the obvious. "Are you getting laid enough? You've had that stick up your ass since you got back from the Berkshires last month, right before the Mancuso thing."

"Some of us don't need sex every night of the week," Lucas retorted, but he waved a dismissive hand and turned toward the window, cutting off further comments.

Yeah, he knew he was out of sorts. And he was sick of being out of sorts, and not knowing what to do about it.

He'd thought about lying down in the grass where her clothes had lain, where the crushed grass suggested she might have lain, and jacking off to relieve the seething frustration in his balls. Instead, he'd pedaled another thirty miles at a cardiac arrest RPM and cursed himself for not memorizing her plate. But it was just fun and games, right?

He'd played sex games enough to know the edge during was as serious and purposeful as it should be, to give the fantasy a sense of reality. But afterward, it was supposed to become a fond memory. Not a damn possession of his mind.

He could have called ten different women when he got back, but he hadn't. He was still thinking about her, the honeysuckle scent of her hair and skin, the enormous blue eyes that had shifted away from desire at the end, when he'd put his foot in his mouth, intruding on their fantasy with a too-close-to-home observation about her reality.

Damn it all, he had more finesse than that. If it was fun and games, you didn't poke at the underlayer. But she'd been so armored, not only in the corset, but in everything he sensed it represented to her. He believed in pushing a woman far beyond what she believed her capacity for pleasure was, because that was what brought them both the most pleasure. To do that for his blue-eyed mystery, he'd known he needed to strip those layers away. Maybe that was what was bugging him. He didn't like leaving a woman unsatisfied, even if the retreat had been her choice.

My mistake was giving you a choice.

She was protective of something in her life, something that couldn't afford romantic entanglements. *"I'm taken."* That meant kids, though he'd seen no evidence of it on her body. Even on a fit woman, signs of childbearing lingered. Still, he was sure that was it. She was also doing it alone. A woman who would take a Harley deep into the Berkshires, who could assess him and let herself go just that small amount, was a hell of a confident woman. On the other hand, that quick, guilty climax had nearly been strangled out of existence by her own will.

Kick-ass confident, but way too tightly laced. Literally.

All five of the K&A management team grouped in this room knew how to read people, but the other four acknowledged he was the best at it. His assessment, based on their short interlude, was that she was tough, determined, and wary of any perception of vulnerability, but she didn't have the weakness in her that many damaged women did. She'd fought for respect in her world and won it, if he didn't miss his mark. She wasn't going to allow anything to derail the forward motion of that train.

"She might just be your soul mate," Peter observed.

Lucas struggled out of his thoughts. "What?"

"Cassandra Moira," Jon supplied helpfully, studying Lucas with midnight blue eyes that saw too much. Kensington's Archangel was what they called Jon. He had a side passion of studying ancient religious and philosophical texts, and a pacific personality that could calm any temper. His emotional radar was as finely tuned as a Star Trek empath's. He also held a dual finance and engineering degree that was merely a footnote to his genius-level mechanical skills.

"Lady has a reputation a lot like yours. She could play championship poker. You'd have crossed her path by now yourself if Matt hadn't had you scrambling all over the Central American start-ups these past couple years. When I met her at Pickard's last year, she reminded me of that Ginger Rogers' quote, modified. She goes balls to the wall with any of the guys, but she does it in a corset."

Lucas's head snapped around so hard he winced at the crack in his neck. "What?"

"Geez, man, don't give yourself whiplash. You are hurting, if the mention of Victorian underwear will get you worked up. I know a girl..."

"Shut up, Ben. What do you mean, Jon?"

Ben O'Callahan, the green-eyed, dark-haired legal advisor for K&A, who had a passion for fast, expensive cars and extreme bedsport, grinned, but closed his mouth.

Jon moved one hand in a thoughtful stroke along the satin surface of the table, as if recalling something entirely different and far more sensual. "I put a hand on the small of her back when I opened the door for her. She's tall, but somehow delicate, too. I did it on instinct. Expected her to take a bite out of me, but she just thanked me. You know we notice women. The details. She was wearing a corset beneath her clothing."

"Devil is in the details." Ben flashed a look across the table that matched the comment.

"What does she look like?" Lucas asked in what he hoped was a casual voice, even as he battled back a baffled desire to take Jon's hand off for thinking it was okay to touch her.

"You're about to find out." Matthew Lord Kensington, K&A's CEO, entered the conference room. The expression on his aristocratic yet rugged features—the combination of an Italian mother of noble lineage and oil-rich Texan father—was that of an alpha wolf initiating a hunting party. "Alice said she just arrived in the lobby."

"Warning, guys," Jon said. "Now that I've got you all worked up thinking about her underwear, it's only fair to tell you she's all business. Don't mix it up with her. She's extremely good at this, and could pull the rug right from beneath us."

Matt slanted a calculated glance at Lucas. "Sounds like we need your A-game."

Great. Fucking great. He saw the concern in Matt's eyes that matched Jon's. Matt was his best friend as well as his boss. No one had pressed Lucas about his attitude, but they'd all noticed. It was time to shrug it off. Worry it like a terrier on his own time.

Because there was no way it was the same girl. He wasn't entirely skeptical of kismet, but the idea of a stranger he'd met entirely by chance, halfway across the country—in the middle of a fucking forest, for Chrissakes—waltzing into this business meeting, was more than fate. It smacked of burning bush, freaking miracles.

He heard Alice, Matt's admin, greeting their visitor. When the woman responded, his reaction bounced through his chest and slammed right down into the base of his testicles. It was as if she'd kicked him in the balls before she even walked into the room.

It was her. He knew it, even though she'd only said about six sentences to him that day.

He arranged his legal pad, pen, and PDA at his chair, though he usually put everything away, anything that he might toy with and give away his thoughts. He didn't take notes because he'd remember, if it was important. Yeah. He could see himself reporting on the smell of her perfume, the way the blond cascade of her hair glimmered when the sunshine hit it.

"Man, seriously." Jon laid a hand on his shoulder, bringing his unusual wave of serenity with it. Guy should have been a damn guru instead of an executive suit. "You okay?"

Because it was Jon, Lucas relented. He didn't compromise business for personal pride. "I think I know this girl. If I stumble, watch my back, okay?"

"Always do," Jon said. "Though you've never asked me to do it when a woman was involved. I'm going to have to give her a closer look."

"Just keep your hands to yourself this time," Lucas said dryly. "I'll handle any door opening."

Jon Forte was laughing at something as she stepped into the room. When Cassandra had reviewed the data and photos about the K&A team on her computer, she'd knocked a lukewarm coffee off the desk. It had doused the cat, whose ire was compounded when she jumped up and trod on the poor creature's tail. It had taken her a half-hour to get Nate back to sleep from the commotion.

Lucas Adler, CFO of Kensington & Associates, college roommate of Matthew Lord Kensington. At first, she'd try to convince herself she was wrong. In that news clipping he'd had much longer hair, fine golden strands just above his shoulders, but streaked with lighter shades from exposure to the sun. Sitting in a board room, he'd looked relaxed as he gave an interview about being part of what had been dubbed over the past years as Kensington's wunderkind; four young men who'd helped Matt Kensington turn K&A into a global and domestic manufacturing empire out of the unlikely New Orleans base of operations. They'd moved to this satellite office in Baton Rouge in the aftermath of Katrina.

Lucas was key to identifying and pursuing acquisitions of seemingly unprofitable plants, which then had a spotless track record of becoming success stories in the team's hands. When she'd searched for other data about him, her hopes she was mistaken dropped like an elevator car with a broken cable.

Lucas Adler was also an amateur cyclist, who'd placed high enough in several marathons to be mentioned in a handful of news stories. He stated he challenged himself to break his own records, always asking more of himself. Conquering the unconquerable. The quote tied into his approach to his career, but it sent a thrill of inappropriate excitement through her vitals.

She'd been bullshitting herself on the team review. She'd recognized him in the first photo. The first heartbeat. She needed to put it behind her, once and for all. There was no reason that day should have lingered with her the way it had. She'd put it down to excessive sexual deprivation, even when she found her mind drifting to an analysis of his face, his every expression, the flickers of emotion in his eyes during their brief meet.

The Berkshires had been one of those crazy things. They were both adults, about to be thrown together for several days, the primary players in the start-up plans that would combine the resources of Josh Johnson's industrial hoist system operation with Kensington's. That should be her focus. Not the overwhelming disbelief that fate had delivered this guy right back into her lap. Okay, not the best visual if she wanted to concentrate on business.

Lucas Adler. A name to go with the hands, the mouth she couldn't forget. At the time, she'd thought it smart not to allow herself to touch him. Ever since, she'd felt like a kid deprived of candy. She couldn't listen to Foreigner at all without getting achy with need.

So he was great fantasy fodder. She could handle it. Even though his voice still stroked her nerves, running through her head fifty times a day. Along with how he'd realized she was getting short of breath and immediately moved to help. A man with that kind of hard-on was supposed to be oblivious to a woman's respiratory needs. Then the crowning moment—the way he'd anticipated her bolting. He hadn't stopped her from leaving, but he'd made sure she knew she hadn't gotten away with anything. Damn if that hadn't really sparked her interest.

It was just the perversity of a woman's heart, she knew. She preferred to control all the elements of her environment, particularly men. Yet a man who could overwhelm her, take control of the situation, bring her pleasure and compel her submission, not only terrified her but made her want him so much she couldn't imagine ever wanting anything more. Ridiculous. A dangerous inclination she would never indulge.

Pushing all that away, she stepped into the K&A board room, dominated by one wall of windows and a conference table shaped like a lotus pool. Potted Japanese maples with their delicate red lace leaves were arranged in several places. There were Asian prints on the wall, along with several Samurai blades rumored to be there so that those on the receiving end of Matt Kensington's displeasure could opt for ritual suicide. While the surroundings might intimidate most, they steadied her, reminded her of the job she was here to do. This was her environment, her playing field.

She'd given up about a decade of sleep to make it so, and was forever grateful for the chance Steve Pickard had given her, taking the talents of a college intern and throwing her into lion dens like this one. Until she'd built a foundation for her own self-confidence, he'd assured her, over and over, she had the gift of diplomacy and mediation, as well as an exceptional business acumen that allowed her to grasp the full range of financial, manufacturing, legal, and management dynamics that made her an effective problem solver.

She reminded herself she'd had articles written about her as well, one claiming she had almost psychic insight in knowing when to mend fences and when to disembowel. Another noted she was so unflappable she could walk the floor of Congress buck naked, not a hair out of place, to deliver an address on world economics.

She could do this.

When Matt courteously gestured her in ahead of him, she schooled her face into a polite mask.

As riveting as Lucas had been that day, he was more impressive now, dressed for success in a custom-tailored gray suit. The white dress shirt and silver tie emphasized his silver-gray eyes and the gold of his hair. He'd have made any woman's tongue tangle.

When he met her gaze across the table, the shock of the contact detonated through her, leaving more than her tongue at loose ends.

It had just been sex. Not even actual sex. Just a sexual encounter. She was repeating herself. Not a good sign.

"I understand you and Jon have already met." Matt was making the introductions as Jon came around the table, followed by Lucas. She could see the athlete in the way he moved. If she put her hands on his chest, she'd feel that hard body beneath the thin shirt. The heat of his mouth had been between her legs, his long-fingered hands bracketing her rib cage, as close and lovingly as the corset she wore now.

She shook Jon's hand, said the appropriate things, and then there was no avoiding it. Lucas extended his hand. Smoothly, without hesitation or hurry, she put hers into it.

A tremor. He definitely felt a tremor. Her color was up. Not enough for anyone to notice, but he did. Under a trim blue suit jacket, she wore one of those thin silky blouses. Beneath it he could see the faint outline of the corset she was wearing. This one was strapless, a faint floral pattern in a sheen of silver leaf that added to the embellishment of the shirt. The blouse's neckline showed a modest dent of cleavage, likely because of the lift of the corset. He suspected it might also give him a glimpse of lace and flesh, if he was a cad and strained.

She had her golden hair in a barrette, emphasizing the delicate line of her throat. Pearls with a topaz amulet made those blue eyes even more stunning. Her snug black skirt had a ripple of fabric at the hem that fluttered as she walked. The skirt was just past her knees, so only shapely calves set off by her heels were visible, but the fit of the garment turned her into an hourglass. She had to be wearing a thong to achieve those smooth lines over her pretty much perfect ass.

The whole package screamed, "Beautiful woman—give her whatever she wants."

Matt's team had an unintentional reputation for overwhelming and charming female opponents, to the point most companies didn't even bother sending them anymore. However, it seemed she'd turned that around, realizing that such men might be just as susceptible to an unexpected offensive of feminine wiles. Could she be that clever? As he registered her cool smile, no different from what she'd bestowed on Jon, he thought maybe she was.

Jon cleared his throat, pulling him out of his examination and making him realize he hadn't even greeted her yet.

"What's the matter, Mr. Adler? Cat got your tongue?"

Oh, no, she didn't. She met his gaze with those wide, guileless eyes. But in that startled moment, like the snap of a gun stock locking into place, he had his feet beneath him again. It had been a hell of a bow shot. He almost felt like smiling.

"Would that please you, Miss Moira?" he asked. Then, before she could respond, he arched a brow. "Matt, you didn't have her take the stairs, did you? She seems a little short of breath."

Something sparked in the blue depths, and if they'd been standing on the decks of two opposing ships in truth, he'd have taken it as the warning strike of flame, about to be touched to a cannon's wick. Withdrawing her hand, she turned toward the rest of the team.

"Mr. Kensington, I'm ready to get started whenever you are."

He'd never really thought about the sheer sensual impact of a corset worn the way she wore it. He was used to seeing it on the outside, a blatant sexual enticement. But the way it hugged her body discreetly out of sight, it molded her posture so that the rounded curve of the buttocks, the long line of her throat, the high position of accentuated breasts, were impossible to ignore. Hell, it made every movement an act of careful, planned grace, if the woman worked with it. Cassandra Moira worked it to the nth degree.

He did listen. He evaluated her strategies, her approach, and was impressed by the level of homework she'd done in the short time period she'd had. She spent little time on the points she'd deduced they agreed upon, then presented resolution options for the more contentious points she'd accurately anticipated. By the time she'd worked down the nearly hundred points they had to handle for this phase of the contract, he'd marked down only ten items needing more work. He didn't think he'd ever seen a negotiator do so well, and he'd been actively trying to find things to break her stride.

"If you find this suitable, we probably need to go over the legal points with the Japanese suppliers to meet regulatory requirements. We could videoconference them in tomorrow or on Wednesday."

The regulatory step was an onerous, information-only process that Matt would typically relegate to middle managers, but Lucas inclined his head to Matt. His CEO lifted a brow, a brief flash of surprise in his gaze, but otherwise remained poker-faced as he faced Cassandra.

"That will be fine," he said. "We'll set it up for tomorrow. I do have some concerns about..."

As Matt began outlining many of the list points Lucas had on his sheet, he studied her profile, the way she held her attention on Matt. Was her focus a little too intense? Was he deluding himself, or was she avoiding looking toward him? A negotiator would be expected to shift her gaze, gauge the reaction of Matt's CFO to his concerns. But she didn't. Not once.

"I think we can work with most of those," she responded at last. "But—"

"I have a couple more, Matt," Lucas cut in. Normally he would have interjected at the end of Matt's, as Matt allowed a pause for him to do just that, but she'd jumped the gun a little. Another subtle sign of nervousness, unless she hadn't expected Matt to defer to his team.

She settled back, though, apparently unruffled. "My apologies, Mr. Adler. Please continue."

"I agree, most of these can be worked out, but we have a genuine concern about stock. K&A is putting a lot into the plant conversion. We want control of the company."

"That has little to do with investment and everything to do with K&A's desire to own the whole world." She underlined the words with a charming smile, laced with the right touch of just-between-you-and-me banter. Now her gaze did sweep the table, pausing briefly on each of the team, before returning to Matt. "But you know you can get your return on this investment and then some, without owning it. Mr. Johnson wishes to retain his majority interest."

"You have very few willing to undertake this," Lucas pressed. "Josh Johnson is not easy to work with."

"True enough. But 'very few' is still more than one, isn't it? We've indicated our willingness to compromise, meet you halfway on seventy-two points, gentlemen. Your demands have not been unreasonable, and I think we all know everyone stands to make a lot of money. But on this one issue, we stand firm. We will not negotiate on holding majority interest. While I look forward to the pleasure of your company for the next couple of days, if that point is a deal breaker, I shall have to go and seek out more flexible—if less pretty—faces."

A text message popped on Lucas's PDA from Peter, who'd been taking notes at the other end of the table.

Jesus Christ. Is anyone else hard as a rock?

Ben muffled his chuckle in a cough. Matt registered the note on his phone with a glance, but didn't change expression as he shifted his attention back to Cassandra.

"We have a penchant for pretty faces ourselves, Miss Moira. Therefore, we'd invite you to stay. You and Lucas can work out the remaining details in here this afternoon."

She inclined her head, though she still didn't look toward Lucas. "It would be my pleasure."

That was an understatement for him. Because he *was* as hard as a rock.

She wanted to say it would be never-ending torment. Had she pushed so hard because strategically she knew Matt Kensington appreciated strength, or because she'd hoped to escape this? Had she been willing to actually take a dive on this one? If the latter, she was already in deep trouble.

Fortunately, there was no way to know and, in times of crisis, or at least the need to regroup, a woman always had one sanctuary.

The admin pointed her the way to the ladies' room on the break. It was the last calm moment she'd have before spending the afternoon with Lucas. She headed toward the restroom without hurry, though she felt like bolting.

She reminded herself this was the very reason she wore the corset under her clothes. Controlled, precise movements, no matter that the mad fluttering in her chest was like butterflies hopped up on crystal meth. She even leaned up against the door after she was inside, as if barricading it.

There were fresh flowers on the counter. White, red, and yellow roses. A vanity positioned against the wall was supplied with various toiletries and a padded velvet chair.

Feminine products, not provided in ugly metal dispensers, but discreet baskets. On the wall, a painting showed a woman sitting at a similar vanity, the curve of her back exposed, for she wore only a towel wrapped loosely around her lower body. Elegant, sensual. Unusual for an office setting, but not a richly appointed powder room like this.

Steve had actually apologized for having to send her instead of Tim, who'd been in Seattle. She was his top negotiator, so she'd been vaguely insulted when he revealed he'd intended to send a man because most women couldn't keep a clear focus with the K&A team. She'd bet him she would come back with everything Johnson really wanted. She'd done that, won the bet. But she was no longer insulted. If any woman could emerge from a meeting with this group without an elevated pulse and the undeniable urge to have a personal marathon with a sex toy, she wanted to meet her and find out what libido-paralyzing drug she used.

On the surface, they were just five men. Exceptionally handsome, yes, and confident in distinct ways, with an easy rapport together. They listened to her, responded to her, challenged her as a business equal, refreshing and unexpected in manufacturing environments. But that was part of their seduction, she realized. It went perfectly with the contrast of what simmered below the surface. Somehow being in their presence made her hyperaware she was a woman. As if they were a pack of wolves who'd scented her when she entered the room, stimulating the sexual radar of every gorgeous one of them. God, if she let her mind get away with her, she could imagine them putting her on the table to share her for lunch.

They'd done nothing inappropriate, not even anything overtly sexual—they just exuded sex. It was something even more than that, though. Something that swept her skin with heat and made her shy away from delving too deeply into it. Whatever it was, whatever they were, it called and connected to the base instinct of what she was.

Even the way Peter Winston had asked her if she wanted coffee. Leaning toward her, his gray eyes close enough to distract—storm cloud color, whereas Lucas's were silver—his hand poised just inches from her arm. It made a woman want to lean in, just a bit more, toward the combat-ready physique Peter had. She knew he was in the National Guard, and had already done at least one tour in Iraq. He had an intriguing aftershave, something clean and spicy, though she preferred the musk of Lucas's cologne.

Okay, so there was no denying every single one of them could bait the hook, make himself irresistibly tempting to his prey. Big deal. That, and they fairly pulsed with the unspoken promise that they knew how to please a woman. Body, mind, and soul.

Overwhelmingly sexually confident men she could handle. But adding Lucas to the mix was nitro to a system already revving dangerously high. If she could lump him into their extraordinary, pheromone-overdosed clan, then her reaction to him would be no more dangerous than getting besotted by a remote movie star.

But Lucas wrested something else from her. Something in his gray eyes seemed to see deeper, want something for her, a key prepositional difference. Hell, maybe she should cross the line, take one of the others to a hotel, and dull the edge of the nonsense her mind was spinning.

She wondered if he'd cut his hair shorter for cycling. She'd read up on the sport enough to remember how his legs had been shaved, his chest bare. Of course that made her misbehaving mind wonder if his heavy testicles would likewise be smooth to the touch.

"He is just a man. What the hell is the matter with you?" *Thirty minutes in a field. You didn't have sex, and the orgasm was short.*

"If you just came out of a meeting with Matt and his strategy team, I expect any one of them could be causing that reaction."

Cassandra's eyes sprang open to find she wasn't alone as she'd suspected. She'd glanced at the stalls and noted no feet, but now as she stepped forward, she realized beyond the stalls, around the corner, was a retiring room, complete with a couch, magazines, and a coat rack. This woman had apparently been sitting in there before she'd risen to approach the mirror.

Savannah Tennyson. Matt's wife of just over a year, and the head of Tennyson Industries. Her face and reputation were known to every businesswoman who'd ever aspired to join the ranks of the CEOs of the Fortune 500, because Savannah was one of them.

She and Savannah had similar coloring. Blond hair, blue eyes. Savannah was shorter, but the figure worked with the height. Slim, not as curvy as Cassandra, but she gave Cass the impression of an exotic princess. Refined and remote, though there was a faint smile on her lips now.

Never try to pretend a gaffe hadn't happened. Just move on as if it was of no consequence, and it would be forgotten, because you didn't make a big deal out of it. Moving forward, Cassandra extended her hand. "It's a pleasure to meet you formally, Ms. Tennyson. I'm Cassandra Moira."

"I go by Mrs. Kensington since I married, but you're welcome to call me Savannah." A gleam of amusement crossed her blue eyes. "Now which one of them is driving you to distraction? If my husband has gotten a beautiful woman this agitated, he's going to be in a great deal of trouble."

"Oh...no." Cassandra managed a return smile, though remained wary of the woman's close scrutiny. Did everyone at K&A study visitors as if dissecting them under a microscope? Of course, that was her job as well. "I'm afraid I'll have to decline to answer. I'd give up a tactical advantage if I divulged that information."

"So you would. And your statement supports your reputation, which is an excellent one. We'll leave it an intriguing mystery, then. I just walked over from my building to see Matt for lunch." Crossing the room to the door, she looked back at Cass. "You're all done with them for a few moments, I assume?"

"Yes, we finished up the preliminary round. Mr. Kensington has ordered just Mr. Adler and me lunch, because the two of us will be working out the specifics this afternoon."

"Good, then." Savannah reached for the door handle, just as it was pushed open, bringing her face to face with Lucas. His gaze shifted between the two women.

"Lucas." Savannah glanced at Cassandra, her lips curving again. "A good choice."

Cass wasn't going to consider what that meant. She was too busy quelling the desire to grab hold of Savannah's sleeve to prevent her from leaving.

Savannah shifted her attention back to Lucas's inscrutable expression. "Lucas, are you confused about your whereabouts?"

Sliding a hand in one pocket, he held the door so it stayed open, nodding courteously but pointedly at the archway provided by his arm. "No."

"Hmm. I didn't think so." Savannah tilted her head just enough to pass under that human bridge, her body brushing with familiar affection against his hip and side, her hair grazing his elbow and upper arm above her. As she passed, she gave him a firm poke in the side. "Be nice. Is Matt in his office?"

"Already wondering why you aren't there yet. It's pathetic, really. Ow."

Cassandra blinked as he flinched from the elbow Savannah jabbed in his kidney before she breezed past and continued up the hall, the silky brush of her hose and the rustle of her skirt drifting back.

A sound cut short, as Lucas let the door close behind him.

CHAPTER THREE

*H*e leaned on it as Cassandra had when she first came in, but for an entirely different reason, she suspected.

"You're in the ladies' room," she said.

"Obviously." When he took a calculated moment to let his gaze rove over her, she forced her hands not to close into defensive balls. *Relax.* She let herself feel the hold of the corset, remember the significance of its support and restraint. The structure and rigidity of it, defining the boundaries of what she could and couldn't do.

"So you're an accountant." She gave him a dismissive glance as she moved to the mirror. "Accountants tend to be stunningly uncreative, if useful."

"Really?" Unruffled, he crossed his arms over his chest. "Next time I get my mouth between your legs, I'll take care not to bore you as much as I did last time."

Deliberately, she checked her makeup, hair. She looked fine. Damn good. Nothing to touch up. Everything in place.

Pivoting on her heel, she summoned a bland smile. "So you recognized me. I'm surprised, as brief as that shared moment was."

"You recognized me," he pointed out.

"It took a few moments. I probably wouldn't have, except there was a mention of cycling in your bio workup. Next time I'll be sure and screen the men who drop in on me in the woods."

"That might be wise." When he flipped the latch on the door, the click made her heart skip several beats.

"What are you doing?"

"I told you, that day in the Berkshires." Shrugging out of the coat, he hooked it over the edge of a stall.

"I don't recall that day very well." Cassandra fought to keep a note of panic out of her voice. "But I'm fairly sure when Mr. Kensington said we would work together today, he meant in the board room after lunch. Not now, locked in the executive women's room."

"You remember every word I said, particularly what would happen when we met again." Loosening his tie, he drew her eyes to it as he slid it free, the gray and yellow silk. As he moved, he countered what she'd hoped had been a subtle movement to get between him and the door.

The white shirt stretched over his shoulders fit his upper body so well, tucking into the slacks. She didn't dare look below his belt, knowing he'd catch that instinctive desire to check out his groin. He was already seeing far too much. Was he wearing the silver medallion? He was getting close enough to smell him, the light cologne and after-shave fragrance that was making it hard to resist a deep breath.

"I don't want this. You need to leave. Now."

He came to a halt, several feet between them. She realized then she'd backed up against the counter holding the sinks.

"You're a student of body language, Cassie, same as me. What I see is a woman who's put her hands behind her back." His gaze shifted up toward the mirror. "Grasping the edge of the counter, hard. It suggests tension, and nervousness, but you put your arms behind you. Not crossed defensively in front. As if you were restrained, in order to be open to my touch."

His gaze heated as he made the last step and his hands closed over her breasts, long fingers on the lifted curves, thumbs on the stiff fabric and underwire of the corset. Her breath caught in her throat and she couldn't help it—she shuddered, moved into that touch, even as she was shocked at her inability to move away.

His reaction stunned her even more. He let his hands slip to her sides, fingers tucking into the intimate crevice just below her arm pits, the heels of his hands still pressed against the sides of her breasts.

Closing his eyes briefly, he rested his forehead on the crown of her head, his nose brushing hers. "Jesus, can you believe this? When you came in this morning, I thought I was hallucinating. You can't imagine how much I've thought about you, touched you a million fucking ways. Kissed your mouth. Taken you hard, easy, felt you come against my mouth and my cock, until you were exhausted and slept in my arms, all that golden hair spread across my chest..."

She'd dreamed of him almost nightly, in much the same way. Hellfire, what were they doing?

"As appallingly inappropriate as that is, I'll let it pass." She tried to slide away from his body, despite the shriek of protest from her own. "It was just a moment. It shouldn't feel like that. If it does, it's because we didn't finish. That's all."

"You think so?"

When she nodded, he considered her, eyes gone dark and dangerous. "Then let's finish it. I prefer having a couple hours to feed on a woman's pussy, making her come six or seven times, but we'll see what we can do with a short lunch break."

"No." She shook her head. "Even if I wanted to, I can't. I..." She let her gaze drift significantly to the feminine products basket, even as she despised herself for using the female escape hatch.

"First, you're lying. Second, you think that would bother me?" Lucas moved with her, and now she was in a less favorable position, in a corner formed by the counter and the wall, his body blocking any motion forward. Though in truth, all he seemed to need were his words and those eyes to keep her standing here, grasping at her fleeing sanity.

Oh, God, all those dreams she'd had. He'd had to remind her. Her nails digging into his bare back, his body between her legs, her feet crossed over his hips, his jaw brushing her skin.

"I'd love to know you intimately enough to know when it's your time of the month. When I'd need to handle your breasts more gently because they're swollen." His hands passed over them again. "Know when your stomach might hurt and bring you chocolate to make you feel better, less cranky. Rub your feet." He put his mouth to her ear. "Women at that time are stimulated by the very...lightest...touch."

Sliding his touch down her arms, he came back with one of her hands and wrapped his tie around her palm, twice. Then he did the same to the other, leaving a length of slack fabric as a tether between them, held in front of her. "Hold the wrap in place with your thumbs in your palms," he said, pressing them briefly to underscore the command. Then he put his arms under her back and legs to lift her, turning toward the retiring room with its inviting long couch.

"No. We can't." Panicked, she started to struggle.

"Cass, easy." As he laid her down on the couch, he bracketed her there with one arm pressed against the sofa back, taking a seat on the edge. "You think the only problem is we didn't finish. I don't know about you, but this is a hell of a lot more appealing than sandwiches. Let's test your theory, get it out of the way. If it's not anything more than that, then what's to object to? Door's locked, and I think you've already seen that my desire for you isn't going to make one minute of this negotiation any different. I'll play fair, if you do. Though with your looks and that fuck-me scent of yours, you already have an advantage."

I can't. I can't possibly handle this. But if she ran, she was as much as admitting it was more. She needed this done with. Maybe he was right. Maybe it would get it out of the way. Was that what he really thought? Why would it bother her if he did?

Sensing victory in her silence, he drew her tethered hands up to her face, fitted the slack of the tie between her parted lips before she expected it, then guided her wrapped wrists behind her head, lacing her fingers so the slack drew taut along her cheeks, stretching the corners of her mouth like a bit. She could get free, but she felt bound. The gag deprived her of the ability to say anything further, while giving her something to bite down on, as if he anticipated her involuntary need to scream.

Leaning over her so she was staring up into eyes darkened to slate, he delivered words as potent to her as the restraint. "You move your hands, and I'll spank you. You understand me?"

Holy Jesus. She was almost tempted, but she managed to hold on to enough of her pride to shoot daggers at him with her eyes. His lips twisted, but his finger dipped, slipped several buttons of her blouse so the strapless corset was visible. "Beautiful. Try your best to hold onto that control, Cassie. I'm going to shatter it."

He didn't understand how much she wanted him to shatter it. She just couldn't afford it. Ah, God. What was he doing now?

He found the side zipper to her skirt and then worked it off her, laying it to the side with as much care as his suit jacket. "That skirt's so tight it should be illegal," he muttered. "You can't even bend in it."

She'd have responded to the slur on her very carefully chosen wardrobe, but he was staring at the tiny thong she was wearing, which barely covered the swollen oblong shape of her pussy. Her whimper would have shamed her except for the burst of additional fire it sparked in his gaze.

"You wouldn't touch me before. Wouldn't let yourself." He drew her focus to his crotch as he used one hand to cradle what was there, giving her a tempting glimpse of its shape and impressive weight. "This is all for you. I'd like to thrust it into your pussy, inch by inch, stretching you, feel you writhe to take all of me, until I'm in to the hilt and you've got nothing to hold on to but me. You think about that, because today all you're going to get is my tongue. Then you can tell me if that finishes us.

"It was more than a moment in a glade," he continued, lifting his gaze to lock with hers. "When I got back, there wasn't a woman in this city I wanted. Just you. I found that scent you wear at the department store. Honeysuckle's Kiss. It's a body spray. The minute the salesgirl sprayed it on her arm, I recognized it, though the smell of her skin was different. I nearly disgraced myself like a teenager. As it was, I got a hard-on that I'm sure made her want to call Security."

Or drag him into a back room and rape him, Cass thought.

"Don't be afraid of me, Cassie. For God's sake, I knew you for twenty minutes, and missed you for a month. This can't be just freak coincidence. Since you're not screaming for Security, I've got to believe I'm not alone in the way I'm feeling. We both know there's really nothing to prevent you from leaving. Show me something, give me something. Do you want me to stop? You like it better this way, don't you? Bound?"

She could tell how hard it was for him to give her a choice. He probably overwhelmed women on a regular basis. But she had to wonder if he knew how devastating it was to be asked like this.

I shouldn't. But she nodded. She wanted him more than she wanted sanity or the ability to face herself in a mirror, this craving desire to be restrained, overpowered by him. The door was locked. She could give herself thirty minutes.

As if knowing how tenuous her capitulation was, he ripped the thong away, going to one knee next to the couch in almost the same motion. He dragged her up to his mouth, guiding one leg over his shoulder, locking the other around his waist so her heel rode on the curve of his taut ass.

His mouth was even better than she remembered. She'd brought herself to climax over the memory a million times, at least in her mind. Only once in reality, the only moment she could take for herself. In desperation, she'd pulled into a park on the way home, sat in the deserted parking lot at twilight, and fumbled open her slacks. Pushing herself to roaring orgasm in a matter of minutes, she didn't dare to think what would happen if a police officer cruised through.

It was just sex. Just hormones. But that couldn't explain why, in a room of available, beautiful men, she wanted only him. Well, sure, there was the powerful memory they shared. If that was true, once this was over, she'd be fine. But even if she wasn't, she'd take Ben to dinner. It was a goodwill gesture she'd already intended on Johnson's behalf, taking the legal advisor to dinner for all his setup efforts. Since Ben had given her a thorough checking-out, it would send a concise message to Lucas. Tell him that this was it. All she was interested in giving.

Her rapid staccato of thoughts stuttered off into oblivion as his mouth took over her mind. Holy God. She remembered that thought from last time, and all the banked longing that had built up since that day surged against the dam she'd created to contain it. It threatened to send the flimsy rationalizations that reinforced it spinning away in churning whitewater.

Lucas knew just the right way to alternate the wetness of his tongue with the pressure of lips, the friction of his jaw, the licking giving way to suckling, then just soft, heated breaths, the feather of his lips in tiny, bare kisses. The limning of the labia, a delicate slow entry of the tongue between them. A caress of his nose against her clit, then a firm suction of the mouth over the whole area, tongue going into a swirling, rapid dance, over the labia, the clit, plunging in and out until she was rocking up against his mouth, going insane because he wouldn't let her find a rhythm, dragging her higher and higher.

Keeping her breath managed through this wasn't going to be possible, but the harder she tried, the wetter and hotter she got. The restraint of her hands galvanized it. She imagined the tie in her mouth would have her lipstick on it. He'd probably wear the damn thing for the next two days, just to torment her. She'd had nothing from the glade but her memory, and that had haunted her for over a month.

He put his hands beneath her, and now, in addition to that oh-so-clever mouth, he began to knead her buttocks, his thumbs playing in that tender crevice between them, causing a motion that rolled the pressure of his mouth evenly across her clit.

The orgasm tore through her, images assaulting her so she couldn't resist it. She wanted to pull him up her body, feel all that delicious weight upon her, holding her down, his cock seated between her legs. She wanted to touch him, close her hands over him, even her mouth. That was something she hadn't thought much about before, but she'd like to drive him crazy like this, feel his balls convulse under her squeezing fingers, the flood of his seed on her tongue. Have the intimacy of it on her skin. Inside her body.

Now she thanked God for that tie, for unless K&A had made their bathroom soundproof, her scream would have brought security running. As he kept his mouth working her, it became unbearable, but she had the wrapping too tight and couldn't think clearly enough to twist herself free. She made the plaintive cries in the back of her throat, clamping on the tie like she was having a seizure. It felt so... good. Almost as good as she wanted it to be, with a man on her, in her, that need for intimacy she couldn't have. But of course, that was the problem with something like this. It led to wanting that.

She was panting, short, shallow breaths. As he came up her body, his gaze followed the flush across her fair skin from the orgasm, the enhanced size of breasts shoved upward by a corset and heaving with quivering pleasure. His mouth was glistening with her juices, and when he brought it down to hers, he captured her open lips over the tie, teasing her with darts of his tongue over and under it, giving her the taste of herself. She wanted to suck on his lips, and he was kind, at last pushing the tie beneath her chin which, while forcing her head to tilt upward, also allowed her to nip at him.

Framing the side of her face with one large hand, he swept her jaw with a thumb. The slippery fabric made the tie slip down, pressing on her windpipe. Before she could figure out how to deal with the discomfort, he'd slid his touch beneath it, holding it away from her, but collaring her throat at the same time with those warm, strong fingers.

"Lucas." It slid from her mouth, a plea. As she arched up into him, wanting to feel his chest against her, he obliged. When he put his knee on the couch, he pressed it between her legs and she moaned against his mouth at the rippling aftershock. He kept cradling her face, his thumb remaining under the tie, stroking her throat as he kissed her, tender now. Intimacy. The bliss of the word was a warning, interjecting itself into her consciousness.

"Hold on a second, sweetheart." He lifted off her at last, went to retrieve his coat.

As he turned, his gaze coursed over still quivering limbs, making her cognizant of the fact she was lying there in her corset and open silk blouse, her hands still twined behind her head. She could have pulled them free, had thought about it as he walked away, but for some reason didn't want to do so until he said to do it. That should have discomfited her, just like him being fifteen feet away and staring at her in such wanton display, but his expression was suffused with pure male hunger. She couldn't help noticing how enormous he was, pushing hard against the slacks.

"God, I'd keep you like this if I could." Coming back to her, he knelt and put the square of his folded handkerchief between her legs.

She let out a shuddering moan at the feel of the cotton linen. A linen that likely smelled like his light cologne. "What are you doing?"

"Cleaning you. Ostensibly." He cocked his head, that sharp profile turning in her direction, in handsome contrast to the soft feather of sun-streaked hair on his forehead. "I also want to keep your scent close, so I can take it out and enjoy it this afternoon."

"That should be distracting," she whispered.

His lips curved. "All part of my diabolical plan."

But there was quiet care in the way he tended to her, drying her where her fluids had dampened in the crease between thigh and buttock, the delicate pocket between the lips of her sex and her legs. While it emphasized that she was spread open for him in embarrassing detail, his hand, high on her thigh, told her he expected her to stay that way. And she did.

As a slow stroke over the clit made her lower extremities behave as if they could quickly moisten for him again, she almost blurted out that her overreaction to him was because she hadn't had sex in a long time. Fortunately, she caught herself, recognizing the weakness that would reveal. The best thing, just like the faux pas with Savannah, was to say nothing about the earth-shattering orgasm she'd just had and move on to the next step. Which would be freeing her hands, which didn't appear to be functioning.

"Lucas." She tilted her head up, vaguely concerned to see a blue tinge to her fingertips.

"Ah, hell. Sorry, sweetheart." Bringing her arms down, he unwrapped her hands, showing red marks on her palms from her passion. Oh crap. Did she have similar red marks along her cheeks, where she'd pulled the tie against her mouth? A quick lift and glance at the mirror showed she was okay.

"Silk is an abysmal binding. Not that safe, really." Easing her to a sitting position, he shifted her onto his lap and began to chafe her hands and wrists, making the blood rush back in.

It was uncomfortable, only because it wasn't. She was sitting on Lucas Adler's thighs, wearing no panties since he'd torn away her thong. The desire to move against the light scratch of wool, against the hard evidence of his unappeased lust, was almost overwhelming, particularly when she saw the flex of his jaw in reaction to the pressure of her bottom. Her heels had tumbled onto the carpet of the small retiring room.

But more than the erotic nature of the position, being held in a man's arms like this was so welcome, she hoped the shudder that went through her would pass as just another aftershock, rather than a sign of emotional deprivation.

Clearing her throat, she tried to sound reasonable. "So how much time before the lunch break is up?"

"About ten minutes." He glanced at his watch, then back up at her face, his eyes lingering in that unsettling way. "As beautiful as you are, it will take less than half that for you to put yourself back together."

"I have no underwear."

"No." He traced the line of her temple. "Just think how you can torture me, knowing you're not wearing any. I can hardly walk as it is."

"There is that," she agreed, shifting. "You're giving diamonds a run for their money."

"Sorry. Uncomfortable?"

Yes. Because of how much I want you inside me. Struggling up, she tried to ignore how he put his hands to her waist and helped her to her feet. She moved away and collected her clothes before heading toward the closest stall. She wasn't going to put herself together in front of him. The slow burn of desire, the physical and something far more precarious, was still licking away at her insides. This had been a mistake.

"I..." She forced herself to stop. "You didn't have me take care of you."

"I love that you think of it in those terms." The possessive gaze moving up her body, starting at her feet and working its way to her throat, was enough to hold her in place, as if he still had some kind of tether holding her to him. "Would you go down on your knees, Cass? Take my cock in your mouth if I commanded you to do it?"

The image made her already shaky legs quiver. She found herself unable to answer without making a fool of herself, more than she had already. As he rose from the couch, she held the clothes in a tight fist at her midriff. Then she realized there was a mirror behind her. He could see her back in the laced corset, her bare ass flared out beneath it. Before she could turn, he had his arms around her, his hands descending to cup her there as he stared over her shoulder. "Gorgeous. Ben would be drooling all over himself. He's a dedicated ass man."

Lucas knew he was pushing the contact on her, that she was trying hard to retreat, but he couldn't let her go just yet. Before she'd moved back to the tile, she'd stepped into her heels again, elongating a pair of already mouthwatering legs. One thigh was revealed all the way to the bare hip on one side, while she held the clothes so the skirt covered her bare mons and most of the other leg. The faint red lines of the silk he'd used to bind her hands were still discernible there. Her breasts quivered, just a bit, from her breath. The blond hair was tousled over her shoulders.

She was stunning, and she didn't even know it. She thought she'd fucked up, and she was getting ready to bolt again, even though he knew she'd wanted this. Even when she'd called him an accountant like it was an insult, she'd given him that tantalizing flick of a glance. A challenge. *Take me down. Take me over. Make it worth the fight.*

"Don't say it was wrong." Bending, he pressed his lips to her bare shoulder, smoothed his palms down her delicious buttocks.

"Lucas." She closed her eyes. "I worked my ass off to get where I am. And if you make any jokes about my ass—"

"Ssh. Hey." Lucas cupped her face, gave her an even look. "What's between us doesn't have anything to do with your reasons for being here. I'm going to go out there and make you fight for every point." He made himself give her a friendly, reassuring smile, hoping to ease her fears, when he really wanted to say to hell with the meeting and abduct her. "Are you up for the challenge, or have I scrambled your brains too much?"

Something loosened in Cass's chest. It didn't alleviate the deeper concern, her personal uneasiness with her more-than-sex reaction to him, but she could manage that. Men often lied, but she could tell he wasn't lying about being professional.

Unfortunately, the integrity in his eyes made the deeper concern worse. She liked him.

"I don't have to fight about it." Tilting her head away, she gave him an arch look. "You're just not going to get everything you want."

"Oh, really?" His gaze lifted to the mirror again. "This is looking pretty close to everything I want. In fact, I'm not seeing a reason to go back to the meeting at all."

She shoved him back, with a tentative smile. "All right, get out now. I want to put myself back together. Then I'll come cut you down to size."

Thinking she'd delivered that line with the proper nonchalance, she stepped into the stall, only to look over her shoulder and see that humor had become laced with fire. "Jesus, you should see yourself walk in those heels bare-assed, wearing a corset. Sweetheart, you're going to make me embarrass myself. I haven't come in my pants since I was twelve. Care to bet dinner on how things go this afternoon?"

"I have plans," she said, trying to ignore the heat that washed over her from his words, even as her heart began to pound again. "Indefinitely."

When his gray eyes rose to her face, she caught a thrilling glint of danger there. But his tone stayed mild. "Okay, then. We bet something different. We have nine clauses to resolve this afternoon. If I get the balance of what I want, I win. Which means tomorrow I choose a different way to make you come."

"What if I win?" She congratulated herself for not showing any reaction to that, for sounding unimpressed.

He gave her a smile that Lucifer could borrow. "That's up to you. For example, maybe your idea will be to yank me into the men's room for the wham, bam, thank you ma'am sex you act like we both want. Though I warn you, the men's room doesn't have a lock."

"I'm beginning to understand why the women feel they need one. I'm not going for it."

"Are you worried you'll lose?"

"That was a pathetic attempt at peer pressure. I outgrew that a long time ago."

Even though she closed the stall door, she sensed he was watching her feet shift, the deft balancing act as she shimmied back into her skirt. When she heard a step, she looked up to see him in the stall next to her, looking over the edge.

"That's a sexy little wriggle you've got there. If this business thing doesn't work out, lap dancing might be in your future."

"Now that's just the type of obnoxious remark I expect from manufacturing moguls."

"I figured. Wanted to put you back in your comfort zone."

She would not smile. She made herself send him a frown instead as she buttoned her blouse. "If I concede to play at all, a game I don't have to play, you've already won."

"But I have something you want. As nice as that orgasm was, what you need, or rather what you think you need for closure, is my cock rammed deep into that tight, wet pussy of yours. My body lying on yours, your legs wrapped around my back while I pound into you until it's all done."

Looking down to hook the last button, she began to busy herself with tucking in the shirt. "I can get that elsewhere, without jumping through your hoops."

"No, you can't. You don't have a man you trust to take you over, force you to let go," he said quietly. "Be honest with me, but don't be defensive. If you don't want me, just say so."

She gave a bitter chuckle, his words scraping raw nerves. "Men always think it's that easy. It isn't about what I want."

"It is, for this. I'm not going to mess with your business here, or who you feel you need to be. But play with me. Enjoy the game." He reached over the stall, brushed her hair, his knuckle following her temple before threading through the soft strands. It made her want to tilt into his touch.

Now, who's not being honest? She knew the last thing he considered this was a game. But he wasn't wrong. Neither did she, which meant she needed to concede she couldn't handle it and walk away. But she'd been fighting to win for so long, she wasn't sure how to admit failure. Particularly not right now, when her defenses felt totaled.

She came out of the stall so he no longer loomed over her and moved to the counter, retrieving a brush from her case. "And if I refuse to play?"

"I hound you relentlessly until you agree I'm the man you want to spend the rest of your life with."

"Well, there you have it. You overplayed your hand. If I agreed you were, the game would be over, because you'd run out of here like a scared dog."

At his silence, she raised her gaze to the mirror, and met his. Gray, steady, unflinching.

"Try me," he said.

Putting the brush back where it belonged with a careful, precise movement, she stared at it for a long minute. "You attract me, Lucas. I can't lie about that, so no point in trying. I'll take the game you're offering. But no matter who wins or loses"—she found the courage to lift her eyes now, lock with his in the mirror—"when these two days are done, I walk away and you let me. No arguments, no persuasions of any kind. That's the only way I'll agree, because you and I both know I don't really have to agree to any of this."

"Persuasions of any kind? Would you like to elaborate on that clause? In case I'm fuzzy on what—"

She bit back a smile again, despite herself. "I'm not going to orate a Penthouse letter for you, Mr. Adler." She sobered. "But I will have your word on it. I know you stand by that."

"Deal," Lucas said at last. He didn't like it, but he'd manage the risk, rely on his negotiation skills to get her to change the terms.

"All right, then. Let's get to work." Giving her jacket one last tug to smooth it, she picked up her briefcase and stepped toward the door. Before she could reach for the handle, Lucas stepped forward, flipped the lock, and opened it for her. Just as his mother had taught him to do.

It was going to be a hell of an afternoon.

CHAPTER FOUR

*F*or the next few hours, true to his word, nothing Lucas did or said indicated there was anything but a friendly business acquaintanceship between them.

It was maddening.

He'd roused a humming need in her body she couldn't seem to switch off now. She resented his apparent ease, slipping back into his corporate mode, even knowing she was presenting the same facade. Only she knew hers was a facade. He might consider it dirty tactics, but occasionally she offered a sneaky bit of leg or cleavage, just to see if his eyes would shift, if she'd catch a glimpse of the brutal passion mixed with sensuality she'd witnessed earlier. She didn't.

Matt, Peter, Jon, and Ben came and went at different intervals as needed, supplying answers to questions, insights. As the afternoon waned to evening, they had spreadsheets and faxes, as well as bundles of past history on both companies, scattered across the table. Initial contract terms were sketched out on the electronic dry erase boards, and they were neck and neck by dusk. Four to four. They'd both secured things they'd wanted, but in each instance it was clear who'd received the best benefit of the decision.

They kept the admins busy, and she'd contacted Johnson's New York team several times for downloads to Alice's computer. They conferenced with Johnson as well, even bringing Matt in for a spirited debate with him where her admiration for K&A's leader increased exponentially. He backed the irascible Johnson into a corner, then allowed Lucas to move in with diplomacy to smooth it out, while she protected her client's interests and made sure their overwhelming abilities didn't leave him naked and shivering. She managed it, proud and nearly exhausted by the accomplishment, because it took the skills of a chess champion. The K&A team obviously would never need the skills of her consulting group.

The last point involved management of the main plant. As they compared people, it became depressingly obvious who had the edge in experience and skill. It was the K&A man, but Matt was willing to allow Johnson's man to be assistant plant manager.

At eight o'clock, they were all back in the board room, on conference with Johnson. When they were done and the line disconnected, Matt glanced at Cassandra. "I'm glad you felt that was a win-win for all of us."

She shrugged, managing a cool smile. "We want the plant to succeed. Having it managed by the best person, with the resources of the next best candidate at his disposal, can only be beneficial to both parties."

"I'd call this day a draw, which is the best scenario possible." He flashed a smile. "That is, if I can't win."

"Is that what you'd call it, Cassandra?"

Lucas, sitting directly across from her, asked the question with casual interest. She knew it for the loaded weapon it was. She did and didn't want to take the out Matt had just offered her, and neither inclination had anything to do with professionalism. However, she forced herself to answer based on it.

"No," she said. "It's not a draw. I'd call that one a point for your side, Mr. Adler."

Lucas inclined his head, giving her some small gratification at the flash of surprise, followed by respect in his face. But what did he have to lose? Of course the bastard could control his lust, despite the fact he'd gotten no relief. After all, he could ravish a woman in his own office if he wanted to do so. Despite his protests to the contrary, he probably had sex on a nightly basis with any one of the women the social registers reported him escorting, another less welcome fact she'd gleaned from the online search.

She would have to accept Lucas's challenge for tomorrow, because her reputation had to stay intact. Everything had to stay intact. The way to beat him was to walk away without a hair out of place, no matter what claw-and-scream-herself-hoarse orgasm he managed to wrest from her. If she could do that, it would be another victory for her self-control. Another notch for her very lonely bed.

Matt and the rest of the team had somehow slipped out of the room, leaving her and Lucas facing each other. Disconcerted, not sure how they'd managed that, unless her mind was deep in places it shouldn't be, she rose, sliding on her jacket.

"Cassandra, you did well today."

"Why, thank you. Your approval makes me all a-flutter."

His lips did that sensual twist, the precursor to a smile. "You'll honor our bet."

"Why wouldn't I?"

"A lot of women would try to back out when they're this scared."

"I'm not scared of you."

As he rose from the table and came around it, Cassandra stayed still to prove it, though her pulse rate increased. The situation called for a catty response, followed by a saunter out of view. A quick saunter. When she looked at him, she recalled tigers on the Discovery Channel about to leap on a herd of gazelles. Those tigers had the same deceptively relaxed movement he had now. It aroused her, just the idea that they might be about to cross blades some more. Fencing, dancing, even board negotiations—they were all forms of sex, done right. But while she'd used sex appeal as one of her weapons, she'd always kept sex out of the equation. With Lucas, she didn't think that could be an option. The challenge in his eye thrilled her.

"You got what you wanted today because it was reasonable," she said. "Not because I was female and overwhelmed by the K&A charm."

He kept moving, didn't respond or engage until he reached her. She stood in the doorway. Behind her was a hall that was a short walk to the admin's office. She could hear Matt and the team talking. As far as she knew, they were speaking gibberish, for Lucas laid an arm against the frame, leaning into her so her back came against it, straight and rigid as her own stance.

"I'd agree with that. I'd also agree you're not afraid of me, not on the surface." His fingers touched her cheek, slid along the corner of her mouth, reminding her of the tie's restraint, then on to the line of her chin, so she lifted it. Keeping his eyes on hers, he let his fingers descend, stroke her throat, using one light knuckle, making her lift her chin further. "Underneath, there's so much going on. You're an orchestra. A slight breath, a flush to your skin." His lips were just over her right cheekbone, an inch or so from her mouth, his breath touching her. His body, so close. "You're all about control. Denial. It's enough to drive the man who wants to dominate you fucking insane."

"No man controls me."

"I didn't say control. A man who sexually dominates a woman, who demands her submission, does so to free her. Lets her fully embrace the passion and need locked inside of her."

His finger was cruising down her sternum, moving at the pace of a boat floating down the Mississippi, baking the occupant in a lazy summer sun. He slipped the top button of her blouse. She could hear Matt speaking to his admin. Jon, Peter and Ben were still with him. She should shrug away, slap Lucas's face, but his finger was caressing the cleft between her lifted and compressed breasts, teasing her nerve endings as powerfully as his words.

"Let's test that control." Lucas murmured it. "Lift your chin as high as you can and hold it there for ten seconds. Then you can push me away, slap my face, whatever's going through that incredibly ordered brain of yours."

She swallowed, and his thumb, resting on her larynx, sent him that unsettling message. But she averted her face, tilting her chin so she could see the wall clock in the board room behind them. "Clock's ticking," she said.

Breathe slow, breathe even. Breathe shallow. Stand straight. Don't writhe. Within her laced regimen of behavior, she could handle one arrogant bean counter. What kind of accountant looked like this? There should be a hidden camera somewhere, a TV show prank. What kind of accountant could do...that?

Bracing his other arm so she was caged between them, Lucas had put his head down and brought his lips to the raised mounds. The tip of his tongue slid into the deep cleft. A teasing lick between the folds, his mouth barely touching ultra-sensitive flesh, like a raindrop rolling down that tender crevice. His hair brushed her chin, her body somehow now canted into his so she could feel the pressure of it. All she had to do was lift her hands to slide across his broad shoulders, or inside the coat, to grip him at the waist.

She'd seen that hard, lean body almost naked, knew what was concealed beneath the clothing.

Breathe. Slow. Even. Stay in control.

She pushed him away. Slap, hell. She punched him, though she was careful to choose the jaw and not the elegant nose or sweep of cheekbone.

Fire coursed through his gaze. For a blink, their deceptively civil surroundings vanished and she thought he was going to wrest control from her, master her in truth. Take her down and fuck her right here on the carpet as a double-edged punishment. God help her, her response to the thought, the shameful need which she could feel trickling down her thigh, was just there waiting, making her even weaker.

But he brought himself under control. One corner of his mouth lifted. "Nice jab. So who do you think won this round?"

She wanted to touch where his lips had been on her breasts. She thought if she did, she would come, just from bringing their two energies together like that. Her pussy was beating insistently, as if it had its own heart. It knew exactly what it wanted, unlike the higher, supposedly more sophisticated, organ.

"I pushed you away in a few seconds. I'd say the round is definitely mine."

"I'll let you have that, because I wasn't watching the clock." He leaned back against the opposite side of the doorframe now, which put her standing between the stretch of his long legs. "But if you make yourself come between now and the next time we see one another, the round will go to me. Because I'll know whom you're thinking about as you've got your fingers in yourself. You won't use a vibrator."

"Vibrators are far more efficient to deal with a passing urge," she said, tossing her head. "Basic need fulfillment."

He nodded. "They are. But you'll use your fingers, sink them deep in your pussy, because you'll want the warmth of human flesh. Because you'll want to imagine it's me."

"Get over yourself," she advised, and stepped, graceful as a gazelle, over his polished shoes. As she headed down the hall, she knew she was fortunate not to have tripped, since her legs were less than steady.

"Cassie, your blouse."

She gave it a dismissive glance. He'd opened one additional button, so the edges of the corset's satin cups were visible, though what was most noticeable above that were her breasts, the glimpse of cleavage considerably expanded. Still, it wasn't porn, white trash level. It was as much as she might show if she was headed from the office to a night club to meet clients. It was way after five, after all.

"I don't have a problem with your boys getting the same view you got, seeing as they're not going to get a piece of it either."

Shouldering her briefcase strap, she kept going. And was brought up short one step later as he clamped down on her arm, turned her so her back was flat against the wall. His eyes might have beautiful doll's lashes. He might be an accountant. But the dangerous expression in his face left no doubt he was a man, and a lot bigger and stronger than her. It made her breath catch in her throat, a sound of desire, and damn it all, he saw it.

"You like the fact I can overpower you, don't you, Cass? That I don't let you get away with your freeze-out routine."

"Get off," she snapped. Even as it occurred to her that control was a very fine line when one was in the ring with a lion, with no whip or chair in reach.

"As far as your blouse goes, I have a problem with it." His fingers glided over the tops of her breasts, making her bite her lip, which did nothing to control the shiver through her. Sliding the button closed again, he smoothed his hands down the front of the blouse, over the tightly bound curves, her rib cage, to settle on her hips. He brushed his lips over hers. "Do you smell yourself on my mouth? Just a faint trace from hours ago?"

When she closed her eyes, his lips moved to her nose, her temple. "You like the challenge of me, Cass, but you're afraid to enjoy it. You don't want there to be anything in your life you can't control."

"I'm not a child, Lucas. There are things beyond my control. Beyond anyone's control."

"But not your reaction. That's what the corset's about. To remind you that the rest of the world may be out of control, but you never will be."

Cassandra opened her eyes, stared up at him. "Is that what you enjoy, Lucas? Kicking in people's doors, just to see if you can? I guess destroying mine gives you a real charge, doesn't it?"

His brow creased. "Cassie, what—"

"My name is Cassandra, you arrogant ass." She pushed him, hard enough that she was able to take advantage of his surprise and jerk away. It may not have been the smoothest retreat, but it was a swift one. She made it to the relative safety of the admin area before he could catch up.

She was safe from him here. She just wasn't sure if she was safe from her vibrating body, her own dark urges, or aching, confused heart.

Matt was signing some documents his admin had apparently left for him at her desk. Peter was sprawled, relaxed on the couch, tie already loosened, while Jon stood talking to him.

Steady. Next chess move. Re-marshaling her strategy, Cass painted on a cool smile, extended a hand to Matt. "I'll look forward to seeing you tomorrow, Mr. Kensington."

He straightened and took it. She ignored the gooseflesh that his brief grip sliding over her skin gave her. Her hormones were in overdrive and Kensington was just too damned attractive. Like all of them. Despite the pheromones that radiated from his every gesture, she was pleased that at no time had she detected anything suggesting he wasn't entirely faithful to his wife. Ironically, that just enhanced his appeal.

"And you, Miss Moira. Though you're welcome to call me Matt."

"Thank you, but I find it best to keep business relationships on that level. It ensures professionalism and keeps our mind on getting the job done."

"It certainly does," he responded, with a cryptic smile.

Turning, Cass found Lucas in the hall doorway, hands in the pockets of his slacks, tawny hair falling over his forehead, accentuating the intent eyes. Loosen the tie, tear the dress shirt open down the front, and he could be a calendar pinup. A package that screamed sex, particularly the way he was studying her, calculating the meaning behind her every word and movement, figuring out how to dismantle everything she'd tried to build for herself. Oh, yeah. She was going to have to hang in there, keep matching him, even as there was a part of her that wanted to run away or worse—not fight at all. Then she recalled his infuriating words about her, about why she wore the corset.

Think you know everything about me, Lucas? See if you predicted this.

She turned to Ben. "Mr. O'Callahan, will you let me take you to dinner? Mr. Johnson would like to show his appreciation of your expeditious handling of the legal obstacles."

If Ben was surprised by the offer, he didn't show it. Giving her a sexy Irish smile, he plucked her light overcoat off the coat rack by Alice's desk. "A business dinner that doesn't end up on Matt's tab. How can I refuse?"

She nodded. As he helped her into the coat, she delayed freeing her hair from the collar. As she expected, Ben loosed it, his hands sweeping it from beneath, knuckles brushing her neck as he let the clipped tail tumble down her right breast. While his touch produced an erotic ripple on her nape, she resented that the power of it seemed to come from the memory of Lucas's lips there, the way he'd pushed her into climax a month ago.

"Just dinner," she added with a smile. "I don't mix business with pleasure. While we're doing business, of course."

"Ah, a carrot to get this deal closed as quickly as possible. I love a manipulative woman. I'll see if I can get Lucas and Matt to hurry this all along, so I can find out if you're bluffing." Ben grinned.

"Good night, gentlemen." She allowed him another practiced smile, the right amount of distance and warmth combined, promising nothing, and nodded to Matt, Jon, and Peter. Then she shifted over to Lucas. "Until tomorrow, Mr. Adler."

"I'd appreciate it if you were here at eight. So we can take care of the preliminary details we discussed. Don't be late."

She noted the clipped edge to his words, and how his attention was on Ben's hand, resting at the small of her back, a bit low. If his finger dropped a millimeter, she suspected it would be on the top of her buttock. Giving her the temptation of more, with the most discreet of contacts. They must practice this. Keeping business and pleasure separate on the surface, but making it impossible for a woman to conduct the former without thinking of the latter.

She shrugged, nodded. Later tonight she'd dissect her strategy for tomorrow. For now, she just wanted to be away from him, where her pussy didn't vibrate like a damn dinner bell every time he spoke, or leveled those eyes on her.

What would it be like to take him to dinner, then take him home? Wake up with his smell around her, her face buried in his throat, body resting against the hard chest? Feel the cool metal of his medallion against her temple?

Maybe in this situation, cowardice was disguised wisdom. Maybe she *should* be late tomorrow.

$$\sim$$

As Ben guided her out the door, he threw an enigmatic expression over his shoulder. When it closed after them, silence reigned for a long moment. Peter glanced at Jon. Jon looked toward Matt, who was studying the stone passive face of his CFO.

"If you wait too long, Ben will drive off with her," he observed at last, leaning back on the desk.

"No, he won't. He'll stall at his car, if he values his balls." Lucas directed his next comment toward Peter and Jon. "I may have need of the three of you tomorrow on this. If you can wait a few moments, I'll come back and explain the details shortly." His gaze shifted. "Matt, it's probably best if you're not privy to it."

"One of the very few drawbacks to being married," Matt noted, but shook his head. "I'll take the risk. I'd like to hear the discussion. We'll wait on you. I assume you'll bring Ben back up with you. Intact, if you don't mind."

Lucas offered a feral smile and slid out the door. Once out of sight, he took the stairs, glad for carpeted hallways to mask the sound of sprinting feet. As well as for the shape he was in, so he wouldn't be wheezing like an asthmatic once he got to the parking deck.

As he expected, Ben did have her at his Mercedes McLaren Roadster, in its assigned place in the parking deck. He was propped against the car door, about two steps too close to her as he gestured through the opening of the parking deck at the building across the way. Probably explaining how Savannah worked at that building, or some other smooth lawyer talk.

There'd been no prearrangement to Ben's delay. Lucas knew he'd still be here, just as he knew what was said about the five of them, both informally as well as in the many articles that had been written. That they were in tune with one another like a wolf pack. However, someone else had called them the Knights of the Board Room, because they had an unbreakable honor code when it came to business associates, community giving.

But the code was much more personal than that. Ben knew Lucas had marked Cass as his. As well as he knew what her power play was about and, being a gentleman, had played along. A little too enthusiastically for Lucas's tastes, but then Ben did like to yank his chain. Lucas made a mental note to mix up the numbers this month so it looked as if Legal was about two hundred percent over their annual budget.

"Lucas." Ben straightened from the car, arching a brow. "Is there a problem?"

"Matt needs us all upstairs. Something just came up at the Seattle plant. I would have buzzed you, but your cell apparently doesn't work in the parking garage."

"I think I must have turned it off. Wanted to give my full attention to a beautiful woman." He turned to Cassie. She was doing an excellent job looking unperturbed by the disruption. Good enough that Lucas wanted to toss away the briefcase she was holding in front of her and lay her out on the hood of Ben's disgustingly expensive car. Wipe every act off her face except the truth of her own desire and sexual nature, a match for his own.

"My apologies. Some other time." When Ben picked up her hand and gallantly kissed her knuckles, his hand curled over her wrist and palm so that as he pulled away, his fingers slid along her pulse. It never failed to elicit a shudder, and even Cass was no exception. It had to be an involuntary reflex, Lucas reflected darkly. Kind of like smashing a hammer into someone's knee.

He gave Ben a tight, I'm-going-to-kick-your-ass smile, which Ben returned with an anytime-you-feel-lucky glint in his eye.

As Ben left them, Cass re-shouldered the briefcase strap. "Well, then, I'll just catch a cab and head back to the office to get my car." She was keeping an eye on Ben, trying to move past Lucas, for he knew as well as she did that she didn't want Ben to get out of sight.

"You didn't mention your evening plans were with Ben, when we were in the restroom." While he made the comment mildly, when she shifted, he moved to block her. "Though I admit I did keep you a little preoccupied. I'm also surprised you didn't offer me dinner. I worked at least as hard on the financial piece as Ben did on crafting his usual bullshit."

"Taking Ben to dinner is a business courtesy you should understand. And I've offered you as much as I'm going to." Her eyes flashed blue fire. "You're pushing it, Lucas."

"Funny, that's what I was going to say to you." Then, going with inexplicable fury instead of reason, he trapped her against the car, closing his hand over the briefcase. Yanking it away from her, he dropped it to the asphalt as he cupped her head and dived in, covering her mouth with his.

He was vaguely aware of the chirp that cut short the startling blast of an alarm. Ben, probably at the elevators just around the corner, had been astute enough to hit the security alarm just as Lucas pushed against her, hard enough to rock the light-bodied car. Okay, maybe he'd only show him as one hundred percent over budget.

So she didn't want to touch him. She didn't want to remove the corset. She was doing everything she could to manage the situation, control it. Taking Ben to dinner, letting him flirt with her, just to tick him off. Well, she was touching him now, from chest to groin, and Lucas pushed himself against her harder, yanking at her skirt so he could pull one of her legs up and around him, put himself firmly against her bare pussy.

She made one of those maddening noises in the back of her throat, which he answered with a triumphant growl of his own when she let loose and kissed him back, her hands sliding along the short hair of his skull, nails digging in.

Too soon, she stiffened, tore her mouth away. "Just because my cunt says yes, it doesn't mean anything."

He jerked her head back so he could stare into her face, make her meet his gaze. "How about your racing heart? The breath sobbing in your throat because you won't let yourself draw a deep, real breath? Just when do you take the corset off, Cassie?"

"I'm Cassandra, not Cassie," she snapped the reminder. "Cassie is a girl's name. A little girl."

He remembered Savannah saying once that men were always boys when it came to the women they wanted. And a woman's heart pounded like a girl for the boy she wanted. He wanted to believe that was why Cass's was pumping madly for him.

"You're my girl." He changed the hard grip on her hair into something different, loosening the barrette and letting it ping off the side of the car as he stroked his hand through the thick pelt of it, moving his thumbs over her lips. She gripped his forearms, conveying uncertainty with the switch to tenderness. She was rigid, ready to stave off an attack.

Rocking up to his toes because of her heels, he put his chin on her head, emphasizing the difference in heights. "See. My little girl." He could feel the softness of her full breasts, straining over the hold of that ribbed cage she'd designed for herself.

"Idiot," she muttered. "I'm not little. I'm tall."

"But you didn't deny the mine part."

"It didn't dignify an answer."

"Or maybe you liked the sound of it."

She pushed back from him then, her expression sobering. "Lucas, I told you, I'm not going to deny we have some chemistry. Hell, if I can arrange my schedule, you might even talk me into checking into a hotel room for a few hours tomorrow to get it out of our system, split the bill, but that's it. The finish line."

Did she realize he could read her? That her eyes told him how much more she wanted? What she wouldn't give herself? Pressing his body against hers again, this time he laid a hand on her throat, thumb passing over the sensitive network of bones and thudding arteries there. "Don't write a good deal off before it even hits the table, because you're afraid of how it might change things in your life."

"I don't have room for you in my life, Lucas. If you really knew me, you wouldn't want to be part of it anyway."

She bit her lip as if she hadn't meant to say that. But Lucas tilted her chin up. "I don't know it all, but I've figured a couple things out. You've worked hard on it, so it doesn't come through often, but there are some inflections in your speech which suggest you came from a poor Baton Rouge family." At her stunned look, he raised the hand wearing his Yale class ring. "Linguistics was part of my studies. I'm guessing that's why you don't like being called Cassie. Maybe the last time people called you that was when nothing was expected from you but becoming some drunk guy's Friday night punching bag and breeder."

Muttering an expletive, she tried to pull away, but he gave her a little shake, commanding her attention again. "The five of us come from diverse backgrounds. But the one thing we all respect is a person who worked her ass off—your own words—who didn't whine and ask for handouts, but managed to make a success of herself.

"I'd love to hear your story," he said sincerely. "I'd love to get to know you. Whether you want to admit it or not, it wasn't just sex. You think every guy gets the privilege of stumbling upon a gorgeous woman stretched out on a Harley in nothing but a corset and panties? And then has her show back up in his conference room a month later?"

She made a desperate sound. "That doesn't make the problems any simpler."

"Well, tell me, then. If it's something I can't handle, then fine. I'll take you up on the wild monkey hotel sex. But I'll pay the bill. I'm old-fashioned that way."

She blinked, then let out a chuckle that disturbed him with its note of weariness. "You're better than I expected you to be, Lucas."

"I assume you mean in terms of kindness. Not my overwhelming sexual prowess."

She gave him a narrow look, but then averted her glance. He noted her swallow, her sudden discomfort. "About the restraints and all, earlier. I mean, I do fantasize, but that's not really me."

"Yeah, it is." Guiding her face back, he made her hold his gaze. She belied her own words with the tremor that went through her at the demanding touch. "You're just embarrassed by it. Don't ever apologize for the way you like to be pleasured. I'm very much a Dominant when it comes to sex, if you hadn't noticed. You think I don't recognize a compatible match? I won't let you lie to me about that. It is what it is, and we'll let that unfold the way it needs to. All right?"

When Lucas straightened, he felt somewhat heartened by the pensive look on her face, the hint that she was feeling less defensive and just more confused. However, he had to quell his desire to hold on to her too long, to try and drive the worry out of her eyes. Taking out his cell and punching in a code, he added, "I'm summoning our limo pool. They should be out front in just a second. I'll escort you to the lobby and you can take that back to Pickard's. The driver will drop you off by your car and make sure you get on your way home safely."

"I don't need that."

Pocketing the phone, he took her arm in a firm grip to guide her to the elevator. "It's late."

"And you don't think I'm capable of taking care of myself?"

"On the contrary. Which is why I expect, if you weren't trying to prove something to me, you wouldn't be contemplating taking an unnecessary risk. I like taking care of you. Is that so bad?"

"I should have run you over with the Harley. And rolled over your bike for good measure."

"Now that's just pure spite," he said, but found he had a desire to chuckle. Particularly when he noted a tiny curve at the corner of her luscious mouth as well.

~

When he returned to the board room, Matt cocked a brow. "So, did it go well?"

"Well, she called me an arrogant ass earlier."

"Always a good sign," Jon noted.

"Or tomorrow she's going to bring a Taser and use it on your testicles," Peter observed.

Lucas glanced at Ben. "You were laying it on a little thick down there."

"Well, I was going to slap your ass as I went by and say 'Go Team,' but you weren't wearing those cute black shorts that drive me wild."

Lucas rolled his eyes, but he proceeded to lay out what he had in mind. When he was done, he had the attention of every man at the table.

"And you think she'll agree to this?" Jon raised a brow. "You've known her, what? A total of one day?"

"We had a connection. She won't know about you all, until the rest is in process. That's the point."

"A thousand." Ben thumbed a poker chip out on the table. "I call a month from today."

They all carried a pocketful of the plastic chips, and now Jon put out the same amount, along with a five hundred chip. "I'll raise that bet and say five weeks. She'll make him work for it."

"I think she'll really make him work for it. Six months." Matt tossed three chips into the pot. "Three thousand, gentlemen."

Lucas frowned, reaching for his chips. "What the hell are we betting on?"

"When you'll marry her."

"What?" He might have choked on his coffee if he hadn't just swallowed it.

"I think it would have been safer to bet on when he'll get a commitment," Ben observed.

"Nah." Peter sat back. He'd changed into jeans and T-shirt. His pose, his hands laced behind his hair, displayed a tattoo around his impressive bicep, the Don't Tread On Me serpent flag. "When Lucas moves in to close a deal, he makes it permanent. He won't give her the chance to find out what kind of trouble she's in."

"She probably won't have him," Ben commented. "I've seen him in the shower. He doesn't have a lot to bring to the table. Since it looks to me she can shrink a horse's schlong down to the size of a mouse's dick with a few sharp words, he's already starting out with a handicap."

"Says the guy with the horse's schlong. That's why you prefer ass-fucking, Ben" Peter remarked. "If women saw you coming at them with that thing, they'd run screaming."

"You know you want it, you pussy."

"Truly spiritual and earth-shattering sexual practices have nothing to do with genitalia size," Jon pointed out.

"The lacings on that corset are tight for a reason, aren't they?" Matt's comment quelled the banter. He was partly in the shadows flanking his end of the table, since they'd dimmed the overheads to make the most of the nighttime city view.

"Yeah. Which is why I'm calling on all of you." Lucas tossed in his chips, matching Matt's bet. "I wanted to do it slow, easy, but if I don't get her tomorrow, I might lose her. I won't take that chance."

"Well, we've all known the type of woman who's walled herself up in her own castle, never realizing she's made herself the prisoner." Jon glanced toward Matt, then back toward Lucas. "Is she wild enough to handle—"

"No," Lucas said decisively. "No. She's first class, and I want her treated that way. This has the potential to scare her to death if we don't do it right. It's got to be gentle, but take her over the edge."

"Lucas," Matt said, drawing his attention. "No one here would treat her any other way, whether or not she's special to you. You know that. If your gut tells you the deal has to be an aggressive takeover, just be sure to weigh carefully what it is you want from her when the deal is done."

Lucas nodded, sat down, and stared at the table. "This is crazy." And then he told them everything. How he'd met her.

When he was done, the room was silent for a long moment. Then Jon spoke. "Lucas, there's no point in fighting it. Things like that just don't happen. I don't care how much a skeptic you are, when Fate punches you in the face like that, you better take what She's offering."

Lucas gave him a wry smile. Peter nodded in solemn agreement. Ben, for once serious, sent him a straightforward look that made the vote unanimous. The bond he had with all of them gave Lucas the courage to accept it, to feel the truth of it sweep him with unexpected pleasure...and fear. He turned his attention to Matt. "I thought if it ever happened, I'd just be in the gate at this point, not sure how far I want to run the race. But I want her more than I've ever wanted a woman." More than he could ever imagine wanting a woman again.

"You just know," Matt confirmed softly. "You know it's the deal you want forever."

Lucas nodded, and then, his lips firming, he reached in his pocket, drew out the rest of his chips and added them to the pile. "Tomorrow."

Grins swept the table, and Ben cocked a brow at him. "Well, I guess there's no time to enhance your equipment after all. I was going to suggest a guy who could pimp up your rod—and I ain't talking your car."

"Oh, Jesus Christ. This from the lawyer whose car personifies the biblical quote about rich men and the eye of the needle."

"That car is going with me to Heaven. I don't care what I have to fit it through. I'm just saying, Cassandra is a fine-looking woman who deserves the best. One more second, and I'm sorry, man, I could have had my hands all over her ass. I'm only human. Jesus. You need any help at all—"

"If you'd put your hands on her ass, she would have laid you out cold. If I need you, I'll know where to find you. In the meantime, put it on a choke collar."

"Lady on deck," Peter warned, glancing left to see Savannah coming down the hall. "Clean it up, gentlemen."

Lucas rose with the rest of them as Savannah entered the room. Underscoring the subject, he noted the way her gaze immediately went to Matt, and how his dark eyes softened on her face.

Feeling his heart twist at the sight, Lucas suspected by the end of tomorrow he was either going to be the luckiest son of a bitch ever, or he'd have lost the deal of a lifetime.

CHAPTER FIVE

*S*he wasn't late, but she didn't come early either. Still, when she reached the executive floor, Cass wasn't surprised that the admin directed her right to Lucas's office.

"Mr. Adler said he wanted to meet with you in his office, prior to the videoconference."

"Of course," she said.

She'd stopped in the lobby ladies' room to ensure she was well put together. Today she'd worn the black, wasp-waisted boned corset, the most structured of her collection. It nipped in and was tightened to the point a man's hands could span her waist, if she let him that close. While she'd originally intended to give her body as well as her mind the message of self-control, she'd chosen clothes to shred Lucas's. A strategy she realized might be unwise. But here she was.

The deep pink cashmere sweater with pearl buttons down the front had a modest scoop neckline, but since the shoulder straps of the corset shaped her breasts, it clung precariously to smooth high curves. The attached narrow ribbon collar fastened at the throat, held with a cluster of delicate seed pearls, which drove the eyes to the expanse of flesh beneath that strip and above the sweater's neckline.

Her straight black skirt stopped at mid-thigh. She had her hair arranged in a twist that spilled down one shoulder again. He liked her hair, she could tell that, so she'd given him a teasing amount of it. Then she'd selected stiletto black heels that should make her five-eight much closer to his six-three height. It was probably his damned German ancestry that gave him that imposing stature.

Adler. German translation, eagle. Sharp-eyed, swift predator. Able to steal away the breath when seen up close. When she'd thought that through this morning, she'd realized anew she couldn't go into his office with the assumption that winning meant resisting him. Winning meant getting through the day and sticking to her resolve to walk away when it was done. He'd promised he'd honor that, but she wasn't so naive as to think that he wouldn't try to get her to change her mind.

She'd also accepted that having sex with him was inevitable. If she could goad him to lose all control, ravish her on the floor, and she could walk away, she could still consider it a win on her side. What woman could feel she'd lost if she was sexually sated? So she didn't have to rely on ice cool calm as the foundation for today's game, which gave her a sense of recklessness she typically didn't get to indulge. She'd go in edgy, taunting him with what he couldn't have, beyond today. Then she'd wait to see if he could take her down, and allow herself to enjoy the challenge. Even if he overwhelmed her, it would be like indulging in a day of chocolate, knowing that tomorrow she'd have to return to a sensible diet.

Of course, she couldn't ignore the voice in her head suggesting that, after the mother of all hot fudge sundaes, it might be difficult to convince herself she would eat salads for the rest of her life.

His door was open. As she stepped in, pushing the disturbing thought away, she saw he was on a call, wearing a headset. He waved her in without glancing directly at her, giving her the chance to look at the man and his office unexamined. She took the brief reprieve as a gift.

Same gray suit today. Silver cuff links, white dress shirt beneath. His tie was black with a thin blue stripe through it. He hadn't yet tied it, but there was a tie pin, which appeared to be a silver bicycle. Likely a gift from a young family member, she thought.

Corner office with lots of windows, of course. The early morning sun was turning the sky rose and gold on the Mississippi, outlining downtown Baton Rouge in a soft, midmorning light she particularly liked, more than the more urban-looking afternoon sunlight, which always somehow reminded her of the pollution and other things stirred up during a city's daily bustlings.

He had the bike she remembered on tracks, perhaps for indoor workouts when he couldn't get free of the office. A large rock fountain in one corner gurgled and splashed water over smooth stones in a pleasing display. She walked the perimeter, indulging in a slow, casual perusal out the windows that took her behind his desk, between his chair and credenza. Sleek flat-top monitor, keyboard tray neatly tucked beneath. He apparently liked those silver puzzle things. They were scattered over his desk, a lot of them the metal bicycles that could roll from one track to the other to prove some law of physics. A family photo. Parents, she thought. Maybe a sister.

The office was very sparse, but it didn't feel impersonal. The fountain, bike, and picture were carefully chosen. He didn't collect or display carelessly. There was a sofa, chair, and coffee table arrangement, minifridge and microwave. Printouts scattered across the table suggested it had been a late night for him. Had he gone home, or was that closet she spotted holding extra clothes?

While he was on the phone, she had an advantage. He was apparently just going over a point of tax law with one of his offshore counterparts. He'd turned slightly toward her and was now taking a more thorough look. In a moment of abandon, the same feeling that had gripped her when she chose the clothing, she stepped into the narrow opening between him and the desk, took a seat on his knee, and began to tie his tie for him, sliding the silk strips through her fingers.

It was worth the surprise on his face, even as it was a tremendous effort to keep her expression casually amused, while she performed what she realized quickly was a very domestic task. Something Savannah might do for Matt in the morning.

She tied the tie, straightening his collar to adjust the accessory beneath it, so when she folded it back down, her nails were grazing his hair, the curves of his ears. She had no idea what he was saying to the offshore manager, because all she could think about was the taut muscle in his thigh, beneath the cheeks of her bottom. His fingers grazed her back, as if he intended a grip to keep her there. While she didn't look into his face, she felt his regard as if he were branding her flesh, making it his.

A quick tightening, an adjustment of the pin, and she was done, demonstrating she was as efficient with a tie as he was with a corset, a quid pro quo. Keeping control of herself, she rose and moved out of his reach, passing behind his chair. But as she did, she let her hand slide along the top, brushing his shoulders and across his neck with her long fingernails, raking lightly. He turned to follow her direction, but she pretended to ignore him, already moving on to look at the wall art. Black-and-white photos, a cyclist's perspective of the environment in which he trained. Speed, blurring techniques, but also nature scenes, a bike poised on top of the edge of a canyon, as if the rider were contemplating making that leap, being limited by nothing, like the Bob Seger song title scrawled across the bottom in someone's handwriting.

Roll me away.

She didn't find evidence of a limousine liberal here. He obviously liked having the money to play, liked to work hard for that money, and so didn't have guilt over the having of it. He also gave generously to others. After she'd checked homework, gotten everyone fed and tucked in, Nate fast asleep with stories of adventurous bears, she'd done some more searching and confirmed what she'd already heard about them. The K&A team were well known both for their corporate and individual giving. Rumor was, they ran bets among themselves all the time for the most peculiar things, and whoever won donated the pot to the charity of his choice.

She passed his weight training set, then reached the closet. As she opened the door, she knew she was in his line of sight, but she continued to ignore him.

Several suits, which meant he could have been here all night. A four-drawer unit built into the closet was likely for toiletries, socks, underwear. What kind did he wear, and did she really dare to look, with him watching her? Her lips curved, satisfied, as she heard him correct himself on a fairly straightforward calculation. *How do you like having your focus disrupted, Lucas?*

But as she reached out and fingered the suit, discarding the gauche, prurient idea of checking out his underwear preference, she did move a couple steps forward so she could inhale the cologne-and-Lucas smell that lingered on his clothes. It wafted over her like a caress all its own that tingled along her nerve endings.

Her father had worn a suit to work, she remembered, before he'd disintegrated into a worthless drunk. She recalled how she'd seen her mother and father in the kitchen one night, right after he came home. Her mother had run her hands beneath the coat to link them around his waist, pressing her face into his shirt. He'd teasingly enclosed her in the extra folds of the coat before nudging her head up for a kiss. They'd been so young.

She'd been so young. It was one of the few good memories she had of them. It made her wonder what it would be like to do that with Lucas. Slide into his embrace, be surrounded by the comforting smell of broadcloth and aftershave, all the trappings of a businessman in charge of his destiny, at the top of a castle with thirty-nine floors.

She suppressed the urge to bury her face in the suits, hug them to her like some cliche movie heroine, but every woman she'd ever known had that impulse, to smell her man's clothes, wear his shirt. The man she loved. Or was falling in love with.

It was a cold shower reminder she was playing a dangerous game, because her heart was involved in this, ridiculously more than it should be. Play games for a couple days she could do, but she couldn't go places like that. Too many competing responsibilities.

Closing the door with a snap on that nonsense, she moved on to the fountain, delighted to find koi with long white and orange whiskers. Three of them were swimming lazily over shells and rocks that might have come from a variety of his travels. At the bottom, a small metal treasure chest opened and closed, revealing plastic pearls, uncut gems, and gold doubloons that spilled out on the skeleton lying beneath the weight of the trunk. She wondered if that was to remind him money wasn't everything.

As she leaned over to take a closer look at the fish, she knew the tight skirt would be inching up, up until he glimpsed the lace at the top of her thigh-high, the strain of the fabric over her hips. Settling one hand on the rock ledge, her pink nails tapping the stone, she reached forward with the other to try and coax the koi to nibble at her fingertips. One of her shoes left her heel as she stretched forward. She stifled a chuckle when Lucas asked the caller to repeat himself.

A moment later, she drew in an exhilarated and startled breath as his hand slid around her waist, the other catching her hair as he turned her in his arms, holding her over the water, his knee braced on the wall just inside her thigh.

When he'd turned her, she had to grab his shoulders, though his hand went to the center of her back, holding her securely.

He was still on the phone, the headset having made it possible for him to cross the carpeted office on silent feet. Now, as she heard the tinny distant voice of the caller, he tilted her head back with a thumb, denying her hungry, parted lips to kiss her throat just below her jaw. As she tightened her fingers on his shoulders, she felt the hard biceps flex against her forearms.

When he lifted his head, his gray eyes were molten steel, his mouth wet. This close to the water, her face had been misted by the light spray of the fountain, though it did little to subdue the heat he'd stirred. She realized his courteous hold on her hair was to keep it from trailing in the water. So careful with her, even as he wrecked her defenses with ruthless abandon.

"That'll work, Joel," he said. "I've got a visitor. I'll get back to you on the rest later."

Then he dragged his mouth lower, nuzzling beneath the pearl and cashmere collar around her throat, and clamped his lips there. Suckled, hard.

High-voltage lightning speared down her belly, straight to her pussy, her nipples becoming aching points. Somehow, she now had the stretched-out leg wrapped behind his calf in automatic reflex. He gripped her hair harder, curling his other arm around her back, hand braced between her shoulder blades.

When he lifted his face, her breath was shallow, quick. He examined her neck, then nudged the fabric back in place, hiding it. "I think you'll carry that mark awhile."

"A mark of ownership?" While she tried for a mocking tone, her voice quivered at the look in his eyes.

"As you like." Cocking his head, he gave her a leisurely perusal. Because he'd taken all her weight and balance, she realized she was in this position as long as he wanted her there, unless she wanted to attempt an ignominious wiggle that could land her in the pool with the koi. So she relaxed, as much as was possible, trying not to be impressed that he seemed to have no difficulty bearing her weight like this.

"Do you think you could use all this manly strength to let me up?"

"In good time. Good morning." He flexed his fingers against her back, stroking the line of the corset. "This one is new."

"Mr. Adler, I know you're not making a comment about what's under my sweater. That would be sexual harassment."

"A simple fashion statement only, Ms. Moira. Being a sensitive male of the modern age, I'm capable of discussing women's clothing choices. And crying."

Cassandra challenged any woman to stay unaffected by the sexy humor in his gaze. His voice lowered, taking on a husky note. "But if I'm already in trouble, I'll risk it all by saying I can't decide which part of you it enhances the most. The curvy ass, which I very much liked having on my thigh, or your tits, sitting up so high over that absurdly tiny waist that they jiggle with every breath you take."

"Crude," she responded with a sniff. "Women don't appreciate that."

"Not until they're good and hot. You walked in here soaked for me, and your nipples are already hard. Aren't they? Tell the truth, or I'll find out for myself."

"Just because my body has an involuntary attraction to you, which you know damn well any woman with a pulse would, doesn't mean anything," she said loftily.

"Like you and Ben flirting?"

"Exactly."

"Did you go check out his office this morning? Smell his suits?"

The flush in her cheeks was gratifying, but her words gnawed at Lucas's gut. As hardcore evidence went, he knew he didn't have much to justify a deeper attraction. While another man would understand that it was different when sex gnawed at him like this, a woman would just think he couldn't keep his hormones under wraps. She didn't realize that sex at this level for a man was the need to possess, to claim. To keep.

This was beyond hunger. This was evisceration, begun when he heard the first note of her voice as she came down the hall. Then, put this outfit on top of it. Jesus, she was trying to kill him.

Down, boy. All in time. You have a plan. Stick with it.

Easing her to her feet, he covered his reluctance to release her by straightening his cuffs. "So, if it's just sex, I assume you're still willing to take my dare."

"As long as there's no interference with—"

"Business. We settled that yesterday. However, ultimately, I think that depends on you. Your infamous control, that is."

She narrowed her eyes as he continued. "This meeting will be a couple hours of Ben droning on with a Japanese lawyer about worker standards and listening to the appropriate report from the Japanese team on the other side."

When Cass shrugged her shoulders, it felt as if they were weighed down by the ropes of tension drawing taut in her stomach. "I know that. Are you proposing to liven it up?" Her alarm mounted at his expression. "You're joking."

He moved to the door, closed it. "Go over to my desk. Put your hands on it and spread your legs."

She told herself she hadn't heard him correctly, though the way the corset's boning constricted over the trembling of her lower belly told her there was at least one part of her anatomy that had heard him, loud and clear. "No."

Lucas left the door, but while she tensed, he simply passed her, giving her a tantalizing whiff of cologne and male heat, before going behind his desk. He removed a blue velvet box from his desk drawer, a box with a white satin ribbon around it. The color of surrender, she thought.

"You know what I remember about that day in the forest, Cass?" His voice was doing insane things to her nerve endings, stroking them, arousing them, making her want to go to him, do anything he said. She forced herself to hold her ground, latching onto an absurd anchor. A children's book she and Nate had read together this week, of all things. The young peasant girl heroine had overcome over-whelming trials and tribulations to rescue her brother from an evil witch. But that witch had a donut-hole-sized wart on the end of her nose and a harsh cackle, not the patrician features and velvet voice of a golden Egyptian prince.

"I remember how you put your hand under the pack cords. It was uncomfortable, the way they cut into your flesh. You don't mind a little pain. It all increased your excitement. The moment I restrained your hands yesterday, you went from hot and wet to full flood, trem-bling on the edge of climax. You crave dominance, but you don't think you can allow it in your life and protect what you're responsible for protecting. Or honor what you've made of yourself. You couldn't be more wrong."

Lifting his gaze from the box, he locked it with hers. "The strongest women in the world have the hardest time surrendering. They don't realize when they do it with the right man, the one who cherishes them, it's the most beautiful gift she could ever give him. Her trust. Trust me, Cass, and do as I say."

The last thing she wanted to do was capitulate to this, whatever this was. Yet it hadn't stopped her from goading the situation with her provocative walk around his office. He got her so charged up. If she put a hand over where his mouth had been on her throat, she was sure she'd feel a resulting contraction between her legs. Her body trembled in reaction to her thoughts, and she could tell his shrewd eyes saw it, the way he'd already seen so much. Somehow, she managed to raise her chin anyway. "The answer is still no."

"Okay, then." When he came around the desk, she wondered if she should bolt or hold her ground. Then he startled her by dropping to one knee, so close it brushed the outside of her leg as he ran his hands down her calves, his palms whispering over the nylon silk of her sheer stockings. He set the box beside him. "Stay still for me."

As she tried to think of a way to respond, her eyes full of his broad shoulders, the crown of his head almost level with her breasts, his hands glided back up her legs, past her knees, along the outside of her thighs and right under the hem of the skirt. She bit her lip at the welcome heat of his hands, all the more unsettling because they moved with swift precision up to her hips, his thumbs hooking into the thong panties beneath the molded edge of the corset and bringing them back down.

Black satin, a simple design, no embellishment. As he ran them down to her ankles, his thumb stroked over the wet crotch panel. He looked up into her face. "Step out of them."

Cassandra let him guide her hand to his shoulder, nudge her into lifting one foot, then the other. She should be saying no, refusing him. When he slid the panties into his coat pocket, she wondered if he'd ever give them back. Or if she wanted to imagine him with them, like the handkerchief.

"Men like to sniff women's clothing as well," he informed her. "Just different items."

Then he untied the ribbon on the box and lifted out what also appeared to be some form of thong, only this one appeared to be of latex. "Keep holding my shoulder."

"Lucas, I can dress—"

"I'm doing this part. Hold my shoulder so you don't break your neck on those killer heels, and hush for a minute. Your only responsibility is to let your mind go wherever I want to take it."

She might have pretended affront if she hadn't just allowed him to remove her underwear. Stepping into the new garment, she had to press her lips together hard as he slid them up the same track again, barely able to stifle an aroused gasp as he adjusted them in the crease of her buttocks with shocking intimacy, fingers brushing her rim, then over her clit, making her hips jerk.

He rose, taking her hand from his shoulder but holding it against his chest. When she curled her fingers into the soft linen, she felt the shape of the man beneath. "What you're wearing is a type of vibrator. There's a bullet against your clit. It has an adjustment that can drive you to climax in a matter of seconds, as well as multiple other speeds to keep you wet, building you up slowly for a deeper, more satisfying release, depending on how patient I am." His forefinger stroked hers, just a slow glide from the nail, up over the knuckles, back to the hand again. Amazingly, her pussy was reacting to just that motion, throbbing in rhythm with his finger's movements. "There are also sensors in the back strap. It will feel like my fingers are teasing your rim, adding to the sensations."

His gaze lifted. "Knowing your propensity for form-fitting clothing, I didn't bring the nipple teasers. They cover your nipples, and through a combination of oil, heat, and tiny electrodes, simulate a man's mouth, suckling you. I'd love to see you wearing them under this sweater, nothing else, and then take them away when your nipples are large and erect, pushing against the fabric. When you walked toward me, your breasts would move with that firm little quiver from every slight movement, your thighs rubbing the lips of your cunt together. I'd have you so worked up, you'd come, just from that walk. But I'd make you keep walking while you came, and if your knees gave out, I'd catch you."

As he kept up that torturous, teasing stroke of her one finger, she thought she was going to come just from that, and the seduction of his words.

"So you're going to turn this on during the meeting." She was proud of her ability to say it in a reasonable tone, even if her attempt at incredulity sounded to her own ears a bit breathless.

"Yes. Different amps, different times. It's silent." He took a small ear wig out of the box and settled it in the shell of her ear, sweeping her hair forward to cover it. "And I know you're too proud, but this is where the taking care of you part comes in, when you submit to a Master. If you can't stop yourself from coming, if you're afraid you'll reveal what you're experiencing to the others, just shake your head at me and I'll stop."

Why hadn't she locked her bedroom door last night and taken care of this edge, about fifty times or so? Maybe because Nate and Talia had been sleeping with her, Talia having another of her nightmares, Nate's asthma acting up a bit.

"Master? What does that mean?" She tried for sarcasm this time, even as her body seemed to know exactly what it meant. Because it had shifted into defensive mode, backing up without her permission to do so, her limbs trembling. If she hadn't been wearing the corset, he would have seen her nipples as large and proud as he'd suggested. "And I thought your intention was to make me come, not sexually frustrate me."

When his hands closed on her hips, just below the tight cinching of the waist, gripping her hard there, it drove the breath from her. Despite herself, both hands ended up on his chest, curled into the shirt, her forehead pressed to his shoulder, trying to get a grip on herself. What was the matter with her?

"Don't faint on me." His voice held tenderness, laced with something far more serious, inexorable. His hand passed down her back, an easy, soothing stroke that she wished was finding skin, rather than the hard shell of the corset. Her fingers tightened on his shirt, feeling the slope of iron pectorals. "You know what I think, Cass? Ask me. Speak to me."

"I don't want to. W-what?"

His smile pulled against her cheek, but from the stillness of his body, she didn't think he was any more amused by her petulance than she was. "Somewhere along the line the corset became about something more than your need to control your life. The binding of the corset was the substitute for a lover's restraint, holding you, gripping you. The way it pushes your breasts up so high, like hands cupping them. You're waiting for release from the one man who can also release you from the corset, who will replace its restraint with his own. Your master. Your lover."

"Sounds like a chauvinistic delusion," she muttered faintly. "Dog collars and leashes."

"Most of those who crave dominance or submission can't walk around in leather cracking whips, Cass, or hang out at underground clubs. They're people like you and me, and it's a need as old as the need for love. In all its crazy, perverse forms."

Lifting his head, he tilted her chin to caress her lips with his thumb, that romantic gesture he did so well, his other fingers tugging on the hold of the cashmere ribbon collar. "Don't bolt on me. Not from the truth. If it helps, tell yourself you're pretending, that it's all role playing, an exciting sex game. I've put that vibrator on your clit because I want you to sit in the board room, surrounded by the K&A team. I want to watch the rigid way you hold your body, even more than the corset requires, because you'll be fighting not to come. It isn't about you begging me to stop. It's about feeling safe enough to beg permission to let go. And I will let you release before the day ends. On my terms."

As she did indeed think about bolting, he lifted a brow, the gray eyes sparking with a mesmerizing mixture of desire and resolve. A challenge. "You walk away at the end of the day. That's our agreement, right? So what do you have to lose? Now"—he changed gears smoothly —"one other gift. I thought they'd go with the theme of today's meeting."

His touch eased, became a stroke down her arms. When he opened the other side of the blue box, she was looking at four bracelets. Cuffs of beaten silver, beautiful in their simple purity, the edges smooth and rounded. On each there appeared to be Japanese characters.

When he snapped them closed on each wrist, they were a snug fit. Then he knelt and put the other two, which were thinner, on her ankles. She hadn't worn any jewelry except a pair of silver earrings, so the anklets and bracelets added an exotic touch that felt exactly like she suspected he intended them to feel. Unbidden, she somehow imagined herself as a slave bought at auction, her master putting on the symbols of his ownership with strong, caressing hands that also said she was his. That he would care for her, cherish her. And she would serve him however he asked.

His gaze rose, paused on her throat then, the mark they both knew was there. "Believe me, I was tempted to get you a collar," he said, low. "But one step at a time. You ready?"

Cass started out of the fragments of fantasy that had taken over her head. This corporate office, the Baton Rouge skyline out the window, brought back the reality of who she was, what her life was. She shook her head, started to back away, though he'd retained one of her hands. "I've stepped over a line I really never should have crossed. I can't, Lucas. This is too much." As she tried to unlock the bracelet, she found she couldn't find the mechanism.

"Cassandra." He stopped her. "Answer me this. Are you aroused?"

She looked away. "You know I am. But—"

Guiding her face back to him with a hand she couldn't shake, he held her there. "Your cunt is wet because I want it that way. I'm going to work you throughout this meeting until you can't do anything but think about how much you want to come, because that's what I want, too. And you're going to submit to it, because your body and your mind need a Master to really let go. Maybe even your heart. For the next two hours, you obey me. Can you trust me that much? Because that's what this is about. You're very intelligent, Cass. You know a woman gets the maximum amount of sexual pleasure when her mind is as engaged as her body. That's the focus here."

For women, the physical and emotional both were key to great sex. Just sex. She did know that. So did he. So was she overreacting? Everything was still within the parameters she'd set. And what had he said? Pretend, if it made it easier. She wasn't an idiot. There was a double-edged sword there, and he wanted more from her than she wanted to give, but she was in fact so turned on she couldn't think straight. She did want to trust him. For the first time in a very long time, she wanted to trust a man not to hurt her, break her.

"I don't let go of control to anyone."

"You will to me."

Last night, in imagining what he might have planned today until she was aching and wet, she'd told herself this was the ultimate test of control. She wore a corset every day of her working life to remind her how important it was to hold the reins, remain even-tempered, clear-headed. What more ultimate test could be devised than one that tapped into one of her more private fantasies? Should she deny herself, just because one man was intuitive enough to ferret them out and she was embarrassed?

Straightening and stepping away from him, she arranged her clipped hair properly on her shoulder, smoothed her hands down the front of the form-hugging sweater. "Shall we go, then?"

His fierce gaze grew even headier as his full lips lifted in a smile. God, like she needed a reminder of what he could do with those lips. Retrieving a folder from the desk, he opened the office door for her, gestured her to precede him.

As she stepped out the door, the feeling returned. Like she was something entirely different from Cassandra Moira, negotiations specialist from Pickard Consulting. She had decorative cuffs on her wrists and ankles she couldn't remove, and was wearing a sex toy that was teasing her clit and anus with every sauntering, pendulum stride she made. A stride dictated by teetering heels and a wasp-waisted corset he'd run his hands over appraisingly as if he'd laced her into it himself. She did feel like a nameless, exotic sex slave, being brought by her master to a public forum for display. It gave her a shiver of erotic longing that shocked her, even as she knew he'd promised nothing that happened in the board room would be visible to the others.

Oh, hell. Enough with the fantasies. He'd promised her release, but she wasn't fooled. This part was about control. He wanted her to shake her head at him, ask him to stop. Depend on him for control of her own body. Her mind told her she wouldn't let him win, while her body and soul clamored for just that. She wanted this claiming, far too much.

CHAPTER SIX

"Good morning, Miss Moira." Matt pulled out a chair from the long side of the lotus-shaped conference table. "It's good to have you back among us. There's coffee and some muffins if you need anything."

"No, I'm fine. Thank you." Cass noted Jon and Peter were conferring on some point at the end of the table, though both rose with pleasant nods when she entered, taking their seats only after she did. Ben gave her a friendly smile and a wink, though he was on his cell in the corner.

"Lucas, they've got you set up in the audiovisual booth over there, if you want to check it and get ready to run your stat sheets." Matt gestured. "The mic's open so you should be able to hear us, and just hit the speaker if you need to change anything."

She'd wondered about the ear wig, but now it became clear. A set of panels had been removed from the opposite side of the room, revealing a glassed-in equipment room that apparently controlled the high-tech audiovisual aids Matt and his team had available to them.

It was also strategic. She could imagine during videoconferences that Lucas's positioning in the booth would allow him to make observations about the meeting to Matt privately, through something like her ear wig. Which meant Lucas could talk to her during this meeting without anyone else hearing him. He'd just added another weapon to his arsenal.

Lucas left her with a courteous nod and a lingering touch on her shoulder. "Enjoy the meeting," he said. She took his words as the threat she was certain they were.

As she settled herself, trying to relax and not think about when he'd turn on the device he had seated so snugly against her most intimate places, the windows were darkened. Nine of the twelve screens on the opposite wall became one image. When it flickered, they were looking into a conference room a world away. She noted the circle of five Japanese managers, with a female translator there to interpret nuances of meaning if needed, since she knew all of them spoke fluent English. As Matt thanked them for extending their workday, since the time difference in Tokyo made it evening there, Lucas apparently decided it was the perfect time to test her reception.

"Cass, do me a favor." His warm voice was so clear, it was as if he were right there next to her. "Spread out your notes the way you want them, then place your ankles against the front legs of your chair. Lay your arms on the armrests. Make sure you're comfortable that way."

She wondered if he was going to tease her with further fantasies, tell her to imagine that she was bound and not move her hands. She could agree to that, for if they were already curved over the ends of the chair arms, she wouldn't have to embarrass herself with an obvious need to grip something for calm. Complying, she glanced toward the glassed-in booth. To all appearances, he was absorbed in setting up the presentation.

A faint vibration shuddered through the wood under her arms and behind her calves, a barely there impression gone before she could analyze it, but Lucas supplied the explanation. "You're going to find you can't lift your hands or ankles now. There are powerful magnets in the bracelets, matching those embedded in the chair."

Alarmed, she tried, discreetly, and found he was correct. "Let me go," she said between her teeth, in a whisper.

"No. I want you restrained, your legs open so you'll feel the stimulation that much more intensely. Don't worry. If someone asks you something and you need to move, I can release you instantly. And so you're not focused on that..."

No. She knew he was going to do it, but still, she wasn't ready for the sensual ripple over her clit, the tickling, featherlike sensation all along her anal rim that made her want to squirm.

"You're beautiful, Cassie." That voice continued, soothing but ruthless as he'd promised, teasing her mind. "Sitting there, so straight and elegant in your corset, your hands on the arms of the chair like a queen. You've got a light flush on your neck and cheeks from your irritation with me, your nervousness, but also from the stimulation between your legs, the feel of the panty stroking your pussy. Do you wish it was my tongue? I do. If I get you alone today, I'm going to hold you down and eat my fill, until you've come in my mouth. And then I'm going to put my cock in there, fill you deep and hard."

She lifted helpless eyes to him. He had his head down, checking his notes, his lips barely moving. She needed to see his eyes, know that he was with her. Strange that she told him she wanted it to be just sex, but she needed the sense of connection.

He stilled. "Cass?"

Had she said his name? She stole a look down the table to where the other members of the team were busy with Matt. "Look at me," she whispered.

When he raised his head, she wasn't sure what she was seeking, but she found it in the riveting focus on her face, his tautly held jaw.

"You're okay, Cassie. I'm here. I'm only going to bring you pleasure, I promise."

Glancing down, she pretended to look at her notes. "Why are you doing this?"

"Because you've had this fantasy. Of someone mastering you, of the possibility of being watched while you're pleasured."

"Fantasy and reality are two different things."

"I'm going to make the reality better than the fantasy."

She shifted, pretty certain he'd already accomplished that. Her movement resulted in a wave of sensations that gave her an irresistible compulsion to rock. As she swore softly, she saw the desire increase in his gaze.

"I want to take you to lunch after this. Lie you down on my bed afterward and make love to you for hours. When you're tired, you'll sleep in my arms. I'll feed you from my fingers."

"Stop it," she muttered. "What do the symbols on the bracelet mean?"

"What do you want them to mean?" When she didn't respond, he pressed on, the voice in her ear relentless, temptation itself. "Pretend,

Cassie. Pretend that you don't have to worry about what happens when you walk away from here. Pretend like you have time to do whatever you want, with whomever you want. What do you want them to say?"

She wanted them to say things scribed by adolescents on beaded bracelets when feelings ran so close to the top, so hard, furious, and bright they burned out quickly, the bracelet cast away, forgotten. It was ironic, considering those feelings were felt far longer when one was older, deep enough to scar. By then fear and doubt made them impossible to say, restrained like her body in the corset.

Business precepts didn't necessarily translate to personal relationships. But both she and Lucas were in the business of knowing people, sizing them up. Apparently Lucas understood her well enough after no more than a day, plus one stolen episode in a forest, that he'd coaxed her into this, holding her on a line between mortification and mounting arousal. The world was full of fools. As she met his intent look, she knew she must be one of them, because she'd never wanted to put herself in someone's hands like this, believe in him.

"All right, let's get started." Matt dimmed the lights further, took his seat at the head of the table, and they initiated the conference. Above the one image, the top three screens shifted between individual members of the Japanese team as they spoke. She tried to balance the distraction of her straining body by identifying each and reviewing in her mind what she knew of them. The translator was a typical Asian beauty, elegant in a form-fitting pale green business suit, her obsidian eyes thickly lashed and sharp. Her long dark hair was bound in a heavy jeweled net, low on a slim neck.

As Ben ran down the points, the lawyer on the Japanese side began to respond, checking different facts as they went along. All standard due diligence for the paperwork they'd sign later today to put everything in forward drive. Ending this. On Wednesday, she'd be on to the next job, as would Lucas.

"Getting bored, Cass?" That soft whisper, and the vibration started to increase.

The financials were up on the right wall screen for everyone's review. She managed to process a question Matt posed, then follow Ben's response. Jon and Peter were studying the numbers, Jon making some clarifying points regarding engineering impact. Her fingers were tight on the chair arms, she realized, her toes curling in her shoes as her thigh muscles grew taut. She couldn't close her legs, not with her ankles held by those slim cuffs. Thank goodness it was all below the table surface. She remembered the way Lucas had looked at her neck, and said he wished he could put an actual collar there, like these bracelets.

The "just sex" mantra was getting forced. Even as she told herself that was what they'd shared so far, the truth was he'd used sex to crack open a layer beneath. He'd taken their sexual interactions behind her battle lines into some deep emotional territory. Her current situation merely underscored it. This wasn't a quick spontaneous screw from a bar pickup.

It was absurd. She'd just met him. But emotions weren't based on fact-finding, data gathering. On whether a man preferred OJ or tomato juice in the morning. Hockey or baseball. If he left his socks on the floor or wanted to go camping on a holiday. She'd always wanted to do that. How would he feel about doing it with five kids?

Ah, Jesus. Just focus on this, Cass. Even if he cracked her like an egg, she'd have to settle for just sex. Great sex with a gorgeous man, maybe even a nice dinner, and she'd walk away. How could she complain about that?

"Looks like I'm going to have to work a little harder to keep your attention. Think we'll make this...adjustment."

The ripple changed to a sporadic undulating stroke. With her own moisture limning it, holy saints and angels, it felt remarkably like...

"It feels like a tongue, doesn't it? Imagine it's my tongue, lapping up your juices, my fingers playing around your ass, making you wiggle and squirm on my face, rubbing yourself there. Your scent. You're trying not to rub your ass against the chair, trying not to rock, though you want to, so badly. You want to pretend it's me. Want it to be me."

She tossed back her hair, trying to look casual, indifferent. That motion jolted a response through her clit, down her thighs, up the center of her body. The corset was so tight it made it more intense, increasing the aching pressure in her stomach, her chest. Maybe it was good he'd spread her legs like this, for if her thighs were closed, the urge to squeeze them together, bring herself to climax, would be nigh unbearable.

The toss had become a fractious roll of her head onto her shoulders as a result of the wave of stimulation. At Matt's glance, she forced herself to make it look as if she were just stretching a stiff neck, even as her hands held their death clamp. She was going to lose. She was going to have to tell him to stop. But it felt so damn good, she didn't want to stop.

Focus. Her lips parted to give her more air. When had her senses sharpened so significantly? She could feel the moisture of her own lips from the cream lipstick she wore, the gloss over it. With a corset, the faintest breath pillowed breasts high on the chest, left them perched quivering there like soft doves, aching for a stroking touch to soothe them. She could feel the air on them, the touch of every molecule, it seemed. Then, between her buttocks... She'd never been much for anal play, but maybe that was because she didn't know it could feel like this.

"Liking the way that feels between your cheeks, Cass? Wait until the first time I put my mouth on your rim, tease it with my tongue. You might be shy about that, but you'll come apart when it's done to you. I want to see you shatter. Look at Saayo, the translator, now. How beautiful she is. Like you."

Did he have a damn implant in her mind? As the legal advisor's drone died away into complete gibberish, Cass realized Saayo's posture seemed like her own. But while her arms were beneath the level of the table like Cass's, they were not on the chair arms. Her limbs were making slight movements as her lips, a shiny burgundy which complemented the flawless skin, pressed together in arousal, obvious to someone who was a mirror image of it. A quick glance at the other screens showed the Japanese men were all adjusted toward Saayo, serious faces intent.

No, it couldn't be... She knew the men in this frame. She'd researched them last night. Part of a cartel who managed K&A's distribution over there, a group of dedicated men known to become suitably aggressive when needed to get shipments out of some of the more questionable ports of call. But reputable men.

"They have one camera positioned beneath the table. You'll notice their gazes keep moving from her to a wall beyond our view. They have a screen there, showing that camera's feed. They've provided me the patch to it in here. She shaves her pussy, and she's got a clit piercing. Her fingers are buried in herself. They have a little bet running with her as well. If she doesn't come before the advisor gets done, then they'll each have their turn, fucking her on the table when the meeting is done."

"You set this up," she managed under her breath as Ben asked a question.

"Everyone knows the regulatory check is as dull as dirt. I thought you'd enjoy the entertainment."

"Does Matt know what they're doing?" She said it in a whisper, not even sure if she'd spoken loud enough for him to hear her.

"They all do. And that's not all. Every man at this table also knows what I'm doing to you."

Her mind froze in shock. She wasn't sure how much time passed before she snapped out of it, but then her gaze shot around the room. All four men were still apparently engaged in the screen.

"They can smell you, the lucky bastards. See Jon over there, Peter, and Ben. They all know what I'm doing to you. They want you, so badly. What if I commanded you to let every one of them fuck you on this table? I could let all three take you at once, since I know you hate to get behind schedule."

Her pulse leaped, as her body quivered in a state perilously close to the edge. She was holding on by a rotting branch just above a water-fall, and she was sure he knew it, for he kept on, doing his best to push her over with his seductive voice.

"Did you know that we did something similar with Matt's wife, Savannah? That's how we got her to agree to marry him. She was so knotted up in her emotions, but we all knew she loved him. So one night, we bound her on a table like this one. We each teased her to climax, over and over, until she was insane with it. Our restraints freed her feelings, and she surrendered to them. To Matt. They were married that same week."

"Lucas."

His timing for such a shocking revelation was impeccable. She was so aroused, so close to climax, she couldn't deny the dark temptation of such a scenario, for herself or Savannah. He'd not only stolen her sense of reason and grasp of what was proper or not, he'd picked up on her fantasies perfectly.

Now they turned toward her, the irresistible Knights of the Board Room. The article reference came to her, and it seemed to fit, men with a code of behavior, a connection beyond words. Irresistibly powerful. As their intent gazes landed on her, she realized Lucas must have given them the same ear wigs, so they'd been hearing everything he'd said to her. She also noticed Matt had quietly excused himself, so she was on display before just the three of them, Ben, Jon, and Peter. Saayo's breathing was heavy enough now to be noticeable over the speakers, but the Japanese advisor didn't stop. The intriguing detachment of it elevated her own response even higher.

As Cass looked up, the woman locked gazes with her. The Asian woman's lips curved in a half-smile, her eyes warm, yet distracted, close to the same pinnacle as Cassandra.

"How would it feel," Lucas mused, "the two of you tied to each other? Your legs scissored together, hips close so that as she played with her pussy, her knuckles would barely brush your cunt. Your arms would still be bound, behind your back. You'd have to lie there, writhing, feeling only that occasional brush of her fingers, the vibration against your clit and ass. We'd all be gathered around you, watching, wanting you both, wanting to fuck you both.

"Look at Ben. If he'd taken you home last night, he'd have wanted his dick buried deep in your delectable ass. Peter would spend hours suckling your breasts. Jon's specialty is making devices that can keep you in the throes of an orgasm for well over an hour. The chair and bracelets are his invention."

He paused, letting those words sink in, then gave her the answer to one of her questions. "The symbols on the bracelets are Trust and Surrender. And Love. They're intended as a gift, sweetheart. Not a punishment."

She swallowed, not sure if she was going to panic, scream, cry, or climax. Her body shook in a paroxysm, drawn and quartered between all of them. While there was no need any longer to disguise her reaction, still she tried, but he was going to be merciless with her. Her mind was full of his voice, Ben's unreadable green eyes, the singular focus in Jon's face, Peter's undisguised absorption with the way her breasts were moving. That first day, she'd analyzed the sexual undercurrent, the way they emanated sex, their ability to take over a woman's senses without any overt attempt to do so. Now here it was unleashed, and it pressed in on all sides, their desire for her making it almost impossible to breathe, to do anything but feel the pounding want between her legs, the ache in her throat and chest.

"I know you're worrying your reputation is ruined with them. It isn't. Trust me on that. Your beauty and intelligence, and the desire you show us now—it's a gift to any man breathing. We treasure it. So tell me what you want, Cass. Do you want me to stop all this now? Do you want me to release you, let the three of them spread you on this table, please you until you lose consciousness?" Another pause. "Or shall I let you climax just for me, while they watch?"

At that, the speed of the vibrator jumped. Her body arched against her bonds, her knees jerking up. Self-consciousness was abandoned, for even if she'd reached for it, it was already far beyond her grasp. The screen Lucas had described was now up, a close-up so she could see Saayo's fingers dipping into her wet pussy, fucking herself, tugging at the silver ring of her clit piercing. Cass could hear her cries building. In the screen that showed the translator above the table, one of the men next to her had put his hand beneath her neck, supporting her.

Think, Cass. She tried to force an eye amid the hurricane of her body's spiraling response. Last night, she'd used Ben to erect a barricade between them. Unsuccessfully, but this time it was Lucas who'd handed her a similar weapon. Since it was disguised as his own strategy, he might not realize until too late that he'd rearmed her.

Each of the men in this room could stimulate her body. It was the same game as always, even steeped in sex. Backed into a corner with two choices, you chose the door that left you the most control. Give the enemy the bailey, in order to protect the keep.

Once he had what was there, he might be satisfied. So she'd sacrifice control of her body in order to protect her heart and mind. The assault of her flesh had seriously weakened the inner gates, but if he was like most men, he might not realize there was a gate to breach beyond the one to her flesh.

"What if I said...have them take me...on the table? Would you want that?"

It had taken a supreme effort to say the words, but she managed to stave off her body's roar for release long enough to fire the challenge, send Lucas a glazed but defiant look. As he locked gazes with her, his face going inscrutable, Ben gave a low whistle.

She heard a trace of Ireland in his voice, brought out by a palpable wave of pure male lust. "If you don't want her, Lucas, I'm taking her. Even with you scrambling that marvelous mind, she's calling your bluff."

Lucas's eyes flickered. Then his mouth lifted in that slow smile. She knew then she'd lost. Or won. She didn't know anymore. Regardless, the bare movement of his sensual mouth shoved her against the gateway of her own control and, despite all the physical stimulation, was the true last straw. She began to go over.

But he was too intuitive. He eased back on the vibration, a near miss. "I won't let them have you, Cassandra. But I will let them give you pleasure. Peter?"

Her gaze tore away from him and went back down the table, where Peter rose from his chair. His corded neck and broad shoulders would be intimidating, if not for the kindness in the storm cloud eyes. His physique was obvious under the crew neck sweater he wore. Of all the K&A team, he alone wore a pair of jeans, having come from one of the plant operations this morning.

"If I may." He slid her chair out, moving her effortlessly, and then knelt between her spread legs, so tall that he was still eye to eye with her, his shoulder span shadowing her body. As he leaned over, she saw he wore a small gold St. Christopher's medal. Maybe that was part of their unique relationship as well, sharing the same type of jewelry.

She pushed down the hysterical and irrational burst of humor. *Stay on course.* She could do this. She could. Follow the body, not the heart. Just the body. It was easy enough to follow the urges of the flesh, if you kept it light, easy. Except nothing about this was light and easy. This was as over-the-top as it got, and it was her own fault. She'd kept it bottled for so long. The moral outrage she should have felt at all of this, that should have quelled any desire she had, was absent. She longed for release, oblivion, enough to hang on to Lucas's words, trust him. This had gone too far for her to do anything else, relieving her of any responsibility. So she told herself.

"Tear it open," Lucas said, something raw in his voice. "I'll buy her a new one."

"No—"

But Peter had already laid his hands on the lower section of the sweater and ripped it, several pearl buttons bouncing off across the floor. The physicality of it made her gasp, the pull of the slim collar around her throat that remained intact. Her reaction rocked her breasts in a lascivious display above the tight corset before his appreciative gaze.

Cass turned desperate eyes to Lucas. "I never said what my choice was, of the three you gave me."

"It doesn't matter. I'm interested in your opinion, but the decision is mine. Isn't it, Cass?"

Captured by the intensity of his face, the implacable line of his mouth, slope of royal cheekbones, she knew it was. Had the magic of the past ages simply been this? A knowledge of a person's soul, so honed, that he knew things about her that she'd refused to admit to herself? There was no way she could admit to it, even after he laid it so bare here. But he anticipated such lines in the sand, and knew just the right form of sugar to sprinkle over them, making them disappear as if they'd never existed. At least for now. "Pretend I'm your Master, Cass. You lose nothing by giving in to your own pleasure here."

Just like the day she'd left the glade, wishing she could tell him she wanted to stay, she wanted to trust Lucas beyond pretense. If she really could, maybe it would be worth all of it, the two of them hurtling down whitewater rapids together, laughing their asses off like kids as they whirled in the frenetic, dangerous current, willing to be pummeled and tossed to feel like this. But she couldn't.

Peter's hands were on the corset bodice, feeling along the edge of the straight, tight hem. His thumb passed over the hard point of the nipple, visible through the straining satin, so close to the edge of exposure. She arched, crying out.

The problem was, she wasn't pretending. She was defiant against his Mastery only because she wanted him to earn it, not because she wanted to refuse it. *Make me believe I can trust you.* She wanted to see the fire teased to raging in his eyes, wanted to explode under the touch of others while he watched. All the wild parts of her she'd wanted to indulge but hadn't were here now. Parts that had been coming out in brief bursts, like the day she'd thrown her leg over a Harley and run for the forest.

She was so goddamned tired of being careful. Logically—if she had any tendrils of logic left to grasp in her turbulent mind—they had as much to lose from this scenario as she did, if it went beyond this room and whatever odd relationship they had with the people on the videoconference.

"Suck on her, Peter." Lucas's eyes dared her to look away from him now. Saayo was starting a moan that sounded as if she were sliding into climax. But not quite there yet. The advisor was finishing, which meant each man would be taking her on that table tonight, fucking her as he pleased.

Peter had large hands, and when he cupped her breasts, squeezing them, she gave a hard, guttural groan at the relief it brought. Another sweep of those thumbs, against nipples so sensitive she felt a renewed flood of moisture between her legs. Then he unhooked the top two or three hooks of the corset, just enough to free the nipples, so he could put his mouth over one.

She cried out again, and Saayo's dark eyes were lost in the same way, both of them giving up their minds to pleasure. Peter had short hair, just a step above the military cut, and it tickled her skin, his temple brushing her, along with his heated breath. Just like Lucas's expertise in another area, apparently Peter knew women's breasts better than they did themselves.

When he paused to strip off his sweater, the black T-shirt beneath revealed his biceps. One of those impressive arms bore a mesmerizing flag and serpent tattoo that held her dazed attention, the way it undulated with the movement of his packed muscles, the strong flexing lines of his shoulders and back.

"Lucas," she gasped, yanking against the cuffs again. "Lucas."

"She needs something to do with her mouth, Ben." Lucas's attention tilted to their legal executive. "Occupy it with yours."

"My pleasure." Ben approached from her left. He gathered up her hair in one hand, using that to tilt her head back, make her look up at him, up the line of his sculpted body. As he spread the golden-white strands over his palms, he gazed at it, and her, reverently. "God, you're beautiful," he murmured.

She would have replied, but Peter moved to the other nipple, both hands still cradling her, and she cried out again, her fingers digging into the chair arms. A flick of her gaze showed Saayo below the table again, only now she could see they had her legs tied as well, only wider, to the chair legs of the two men on either side of her. Each had a hand high on her thigh, adding to the sensation of being held open.

A series of symbols were tattooed on the inside of the one thigh. Cass realized two of them were the same as those on her bracelets, but her mind couldn't process which two they might be, or what the others might signify. Though that dark part of her that Lucas had tapped knew intuitively it was some mark of ownership, that Saayo willingly belonged to at least one of the men in that room.

Ben had wrapped her hair around his broad palm again and was descending, his firm mouth, green eyes coming down, his grip strong, sure. Not hurried. She was overwhelmed by the sensation of being desired, of their need to savor her, one luscious bite at a time. As if reflecting her thoughts, Peter nipped at her. She screamed at the resulting wave of sensation that took her over. Then there was the heat of Ben's breath. His kiss would be like everything else here. Pure blow-the-top-off-her-world fantasy.

But not bliss, not a resting place for her heart, which was what Lucas's kiss had seemed to offer. She couldn't risk herself on the illusion or the truth of that. But this, Ben's kiss, this was just the physical. What she knew was safe. What she could accept.

As Ben's hand cradled her jaw, his thumb brushing her cheek—yes, they all definitely knew how to make a woman melt—she surrendered.

She averted her face.

CHAPTER SEVEN

*S*he pressed it into her shoulder, her breath fast and shallow, tiny whimpers coming from her throat just above Peter's ministrations, her body jerking in pre-orgasmic spasms. She couldn't tell Lucas she needed to stop. Not because she was about to climax, but because she was about to plummet over a far worse precipice.

But at that gesture, Peter sat back on his heels and Ben straightened, signal apparently received. When Saayo came to climax then, a long, yearning cry, the shuddering thrill of it rippled through her own pussy, her body jerking again as Peter gently rearranged the corset cups back over her breasts. Ben threaded a hand through her hair once more, a stroke of reassurance as he leaned over her and laid her hair comb on the table. Then, unexpectedly, he eased her sweater off one shoulder. She trembled as she saw him register Lucas's mark on her throat, a moment before he placed his lips on her bare skin, several inches away from that possessive brand. Then he eased the fabric back in place and withdrew.

She closed her eyes. What had she done? It was a game. Only a game. She'd scoffed at the idea that emotions like this could exist after just meeting someone. But she'd just turned from the penultimate sexual experience. Where Peter's lips on her breasts and being watched by a group of near strangers while she was brought to climax had been, remarkably, something she could handle, the intimacy of lips, of Ben's mouth, was not. She was far too aware that if it had been Lucas's mouth, she would have been okay.

"Cassie, open your eyes."

She didn't know how long she'd kept them closed, but when she raised her lashes, she found the room silent, the video screen dark. They were alone and Lucas was standing before her. He studied her, unsmiling, leaning against the table only a couple feet away.

She had to tilt her face to see him and the disadvantage, while uncomfortable, didn't match the abrupt, inexplicable desire she had to go onto her knees before him, take him into her mouth, serve him. For her own comfort. Something was wrong with her. She was tired. Too tired.

"Ssh." Instead, he dropped to one knee before her and laid his hand on her cheek, much as Ben had. She shuddered with emotion, beyond mere physical reaction. "I'm going to make you come. Would you like that?"

She nodded. "Would you have…"

He offered a strained smile. She had such a desire to reach out and feather her fingers through that scattering of blond hair across his high forehead, trace the thoughtful lines that had formed there. "I didn't expect it to become that intense," he admitted. "Though I suspected it was possible. I knew there was more between us than sex. You're an incredibly hot woman, Cass. Makes a man who wants you do crazy things. Obviously." That tug of a smile again.

"The answer is no, though. I would have stopped Ben a second before he kissed you. I didn't want to see his mouth on you. Or let him touch you. Maybe Matt and I are different, or maybe it's that our relationship to Savannah and him is different. He's…"

"He's the leader. Like a king to his soldiers. You all serve him, in a way."

"Sounds pretty ridiculous in the modern world, doesn't it?"

Glancing down, she experienced a weary but wry smile herself. "Can't really speak to that. And Peter?"

"Well, Peter's different." Lucas lifted a shoulder. "He has this thing about breasts. You can't really deny him a taste. It's like denying a puppy a treat or something. He gets the soulful eyes going, and you just feel like shit."

She coughed, a surprised laugh, but then she had to swallow it, for he surged up and seized her mouth with his. So forcefully, he knocked the chair back, pushing it off its front legs into a tilt against the table, his hands clamped over her wrists as he leaned over her. She used his mouth to breathe, because her breath was gone. Catching her hair, he moved down her throat, adding another bite to that sensitive mark, tongued the cleft between her breasts as she whimpered anew, and then he dropped down again, keeping the chair tilted up with one knee beneath it, his gaze zeroed in between her legs.

The panty detached from the side, and he slid it out from under her, tossing it to the side. "If you come, it's going to be my mouth, my hand, my cock. You understand? No offense to Jon's wizardry, but I want your response to be because of my touch, always."

She nodded, trying to ignore the last word and the butterflies it gave her. "Please, do it now. All I've been thinking about is your mouth there." That and his cock, but she knew that was truly the point of no return.

The flame in his eyes was as gratifying as she'd feared it would be. Unzipping the back of her skirt, he pushed it up and out of the way before grasping her hips, cupping her buttocks, and lifted her to a different tilt. His golden hair brushed her thighs as his tongue slid into her, his mouth sweeping over her clit and labia.

She expected to come just at the thought of his mouth on her, but he surprised her with his knowledge of a woman's body again. Slowing the pace, teasing the hypersensitivity of her engorged flesh, he indulged in brief touches, tantalizing licks, nothing rhythmic or too much, so he actually took her down a notch. The searing pain of a raging burn changed into a swirling, slow yearning that began to build, not like a tornado, but a tropical storm, its advance slow but unstoppable. He held her on that point, spiraling up, until tiny cries were coming from her, pleading, as time ticked away and she knew her mind was lost forever. She'd become all sensation, nothing else.

At length, he pressed his lips to her thigh, making her register the fact she was shaking all over. "If I was in your bed, Cass," he whispered, "I'd lace you into your corset every morning, making it as tight as I pleased. You'd wear it at my pleasure, and you'd wear it to remember you belong to me. That's one of the main reasons you wear it now, isn't it? Imagining that you wear it for a man?"

A quick jerk of her head was all she could summon. No point in denying anything, for everything but truth was stripped away. She hadn't really acknowledged the truth of it herself until he showed it to her. A man she was all too willing to allow to master her. His eyes flashed. "So there you go, then. You don't think it's just sex between us anymore, do you?"

"You...know lots of things about women," she hedged. "All of you."

He nodded. "We do know lots about women. Enough that we know every one of them is a mystery, and those mysteries overlap, give us an avenue into the heart of the next treasure to unravel. But you're different. You're a mystery, Cassie, but from the moment I saw you in the glade, I knew there was a part of you that was open to me uniquely, clear as the blue sky, like your gorgeous eyes. So full of arousal, so worried. You're meant to be appreciated and cherished every day, just like that sky. Doesn't matter to me whether it's cloudy, sunny, or storm dark. You know me, too. The same way. That's why you make me crazy like this. Time has nothing to do with it."

Lowering his head, he put his mouth on her again. Sliding his hands beneath her hips, he began to move her in a rhythm against him, fingers teasing the cleft between her buttocks again, reawakening all the nerves provoked by the earlier vibration.

Her head dropped back, snapped forward, the only part of her that could move with abandon, and she thrashed with it now, her blond hair sweeping over the satin mahogany finish of the table. Her movements whipped some of the strands across her mouth, then they fell away again. Unbidden, she imagined what it would have been like, having them all in here watching Lucas do this to her, claim her this way, with his mouth, with his ability to bring her to climax. A fantasy with a medieval flare to it, the bedding of the bride.

Marking his claim upon her as Matt had done Savannah. She pictured it as a dark and stormy night they had done that, the room dim like this, filled with the watchful stillness of aroused men, a woman's rasping breath like Saayo's, one man's eyes watching her every movement, knowing just when to move in and take her up to screaming climax before them all, calling his name.

Maybe an hour or two ago she'd have been flummoxed by this, as well as Matt's relationship to his wife. She lived in a modern world where female independence was so strategically critical, and yet now it fit, made sense to her in a way that was entirely illogical, inexplicable. She'd say it was hormones, but he'd just given her an example that it wasn't. Not only in her desire not to be kissed by anyone but him, but in the apparently successful marriage between two people highly respected in the business world.

"First time in my mouth. Next time for my cock." Raising his head, he dug his fingers into her legs. "You will have lunch with me today, and then I'm going to take you somewhere, fuck you, and make you completely mine."

"Yes. Yes." She couldn't think about all the reasons that wasn't likely to happen.

She just needed him now and she, the paragon of business integrity, would lie, steal, cheat—hell, maybe even kill, if it was some psycho criminal who deserved it—to have him consider her his, to belong to him, heart, soul, and mind, for at least these few minutes. She'd give herself this, even if it tarnished her to do it.

He held her gaze, though. "I won't let you lie to me, Cassie. It will happen, even if you try to back out."

She'd never heard more reassuring words, even knowing he'd likely be the one backing out. "Please, Lucas."

He nodded, lowered his attention again, and his mouth breathed on her.

"Oh, God." She strained against her bonds.

"Beg, Cassandra. Make it dirty. Ask for it the way I know you want it."

"Please...make me come. I want my pussy, hard against your face. I want to see my come on your mouth, your cheeks, know that you've rubbed your face all in it. I want your tongue fucking me."

And she let out a cry as he did just that, working into her, teasing her inside and out, his fingers tight, bruising, yanking her forward against her bonds to shove her against his face, making the chair rap against the table once before he let out an oath, pressed a control beneath the chair, freeing her arms and legs. But she didn't want to be free.

Picking her up under the arms, he lifted her as if she weighed nothing, brought her down on the table, guiding her arms above her head. The magnets in the restraints clamped to each other as he crossed her wrists and left them there. Pulling her hips off the end of the table, he returned to his penetration of her, the wild licking of her clit and labia in a way that seemed to have no rhyme or reason but was bringing her to a sure, spiraling release.

When it happened, she screamed long, heels hitting his back, her hips beating on the table, the world flashing with spots and colors. As she fought for air, she welcomed the stranglehold of the corset, of his restraints, of the brutal force of his hands. Her breasts were generous, milky white overflowing curves that drew and held his fascinated gaze. If things ended between them, as she knew they would, it would be months, maybe years, before she got it out of her head, the idea he'd placed there. That the restraint of the corset was his restraint upon her. That she wore it for him. For the hope of a man like him.

She'd seen the fetish sites, her fantasies depicted in such a demeaning way she'd never allowed herself to think of it as more than a guilty private depravity that crept in when she sought to relieve her own frustration. Even then, in the aftermath, she'd passed it off as a typical woman's desire to be ravished by a forceful alpha male, nothing darker and needier than that.

But Lucas had opened up a different take on that world, one that could exist in the real world, that was gilded with the light of her true desires. In that world, he could stake his claim and not only bring her this kind of ecstasy, but give her a shelter in the storm.

Those embarrassing trappings of overly made up porn actresses with whips and leather corsets fell away from what it really meant. Protection and devotion. Belonging.

Trust, surrender, and love. The bracelets. Oh, God, she was losing her mind.

She wasn't sure if she lost consciousness, but she might have. All she knew was when she tuned back in, she was no longer on the table. Lucas was on the floor, sitting on the cushioned carpet, his back against the wall. He was holding her in his lap, toying with those three open hooks of her corset, making brief caresses of her exposed nipples that increased her trembling. He'd rearranged her skirt, though, and her shoes were neatly paired next to the two of them, waiting for her.

As he looked down at her, his eyes were filled with so many things, she found she couldn't think of what to say to him. With her emotions in a jumble, her mind fled into the refuge of numb shock.

But he spoke first. "I believe you have to let me take you to lunch now."

~

He wouldn't let her throw herself out the window instead of walking through the admin's office, where she could hear the other men talking. Since her sweater was stripped of buttons, he removed his dress shirt, under which he wore a white T-shirt, and put it on her, rolling up the sleeves. Though too large, it gave her an Annie Hall look that was reasonably fashionable over her dark skirt. She was coated in his scent. He wouldn't let her have her hair clip back, for he told her he wanted the corn silk of her hair spread out on her shoulders. As he examined her, he let his finger dip into the neckline of the shirt, unbuttoned to the point he could tease the cleft between her breasts, the top refastened hooks of her corset.

"You shouldn't look like you won the war." She was proud when she found her voice at last. "Just a battle."

He'd told her she was different than other women he'd seduced. She was determined to act like it, even as she refused to let herself acknowledge the jealousy she felt about those others. It was misplaced, regardless, for he likely owed his incredible expertise to practice sessions with them.

"I'll look forward to any battle with you." His eyes were warm and distracting as they coursed over her, but then he surprised her by removing the bracelets with caressing hands. As he dropped to do the same with the anklets, he must have seen something that betrayed her surprisingly bereft reaction, for he dropped a kiss along the inside of her knee, making her shiver. He rose. "They're yours, sweetheart, but you have to ask for them back. And when you do, it will be because you've accepted you're mine. Let's go."

Whether it was the shock of digesting those words or the fact he'd reminded her she was about to go back in front of the team, she didn't realize she'd planted her feet until she rocked against his tug on her hand. Since she was wearing the tall heels again, he was courteous enough not to yank. But he turned around, put both hands on her shoulders, leaning in so she had to meet his gaze and smell her own scent on his firm mouth. "Cass, this won't be bad, I promise. When a woman embraces her sexual desires, it doesn't place a mark against her intelligence or our respect for her. We don't share the crude and immature way our society views sex."

"Sure you don't." She struggled to find her tongue. "A bunch of guys—you're all above that."

A flash of teeth. "I didn't say we don't appreciate a naked female. But we appreciate her differently. At one time, most of us were as typical about it as you'd expect. But Jon taught us an alternative perspective. It's a sacred act, a gift you've given us tonight. C'mon. Trust me."

With a little more coaxing on the same line, along with a half-teasing threat to just ravish her on the floor if she didn't move her ass, he was finally able to get her walking toward the front office area. She told herself the whole way she wouldn't bolt, though not doing so was one of the hardest things she'd ever done. Which, considering her past, was saying a great deal.

When they stepped into the room, her heart jumped into her throat as they all turned. However, Peter was closest, and he stepped to her immediately, drawing her away from Lucas and astonishing her with a strong-armed, reassuring hug, his body a hard bulwark against any shame or guilt. Absurdly, almost like a big brother. As he eased her back, he grinned down at her, as if the two of them were part of a planned conspiracy. "That was the best damn regulatory review I've ever attended. Think we should do that more often."

"In your dreams," Lucas said dryly.

Jon came next. Kissing her hand, he gave her a pleased, gentle smile. "When you feel comfortable about it, Miss Moira, I'd like to know how the device and the chair worked for you. I know it's no comparison to Lucas's devil-blessed mouth, but I like to improve my work."

"Sure," she said faintly. He squeezed her hand. Ben had drawn close, giving her a friendly, concerned look. They were grouped around her, Lucas at her back. Amusingly, she felt adopted, in a very non-sibling way.

Being the oldest sibling in her own family, she knew what it was to offer reassurance and protection to others, guidance, shelter. Just like the remarkable idea of Lucas's feelings for her after such a short time, this had an intuitive feel to it, a relationship meant to be, waiting out there in the collective consciousness until they were brought into the same room, under these unusual circumstances.

"You all seem...very comfortable with this." She groped for something to say.

Ben took her hands then, pulling her to him. He gave her a hug, too, though his hands wandered over her with regret, until Lucas made a warning growl in his throat that did remind her of wolves. Ben lifted his head, his eyes twinkling. "You need to know we don't make a habit of ravishing our female associates. You're a special case. As Lucas told you, Savannah has been the only other one. I'll let you draw your own conclusions for that."

Then he stepped back and she saw Matt Kensington sitting on the arm of the couch, watching them all. When he rose, holding out a hand, Lucas touched her back, a reassurance as she moved forward, putting her hand with only a slight hesitation into Matt's.

"With the exception of my own wife, I've never met a more clever businesswoman. If Steve Pickard didn't have my utmost respect, I'd steal you from him. Plus, I can tell you have an integrity that can't be bought."

"No, sir. Mr. Kensington."

He squeezed her fingers. The hawklike dark eyes studied her, his sensuous mouth in a thoughtful line. She'd tried not to notice those things too closely, given that he was married, but now she noticed it all, including his commanding grip, telling her what kind of animal she was dealing with. She saw it, too, in the way his gaze flickered when she addressed him formally.

As it dawned on her, she looked around her, saw that same brand of sexual dominance stamped on every one of them, even the gentle Jon, and comprehended another element that gave them their understanding of one another. It was a heady combination, one that made her more cognizant of how she'd been drawn into the fantasy so easily. But that emphasized it had to be a fantasy, a few stolen moments. If she was wise, she'd start shoring up her defenses.

"I feel like the cheerleader who gets protected by the whole football team," she ventured. "Not sure whether to feel offended or just amused."

She couldn't deny the gratification she felt at Matt's smile, though. "We are unapologetically male, Cassandra. I look forward to seeing you bust Lucas's balls regularly. He needs it. Arrogance is an unfortunate trait."

"Really?" She arched a brow. "It's so fortunate, then, that the rest of you don't goad him by example."

A feminine chuckle showed Savannah in the doorway. "Truer words," she said lightly.

It was like a family gathering, one that made the low-level yearning simmering in her gut expand to a more painful size. This sense of belonging wasn't for her. She couldn't keep it.

"I need to go," she said abruptly. When she noted her briefcase was next to Matt, he beat her to it, but simply handed it to her. Though his smile had given her a rewarding sense of pleasure, his quiet and shrewd expression now was something she avoided. She cleared her throat, drew herself up, and swept a glance over all of them, lingering on none. She didn't turn to face Lucas yet, still a weighted presence behind her.

"I...this has been a profound experience, for certain, but obviously my work is done here. The remaining paperwork can be tied up via fax and e-mail. Thank you, Mr. Kensington. Mr. Johnson will be very pleased."

She nodded blindly to the men, moving through them, hoping none would shift to stop her, somehow wishing they would. A corset was no protection against these kind of forces. It was a damn liability.

When she reached Savannah, the woman's expression, like her husband's, held a knowledge that terrified Cass.

"I know just how you feel," Matt's wife murmured, with a poignant smile. "Run. He'll catch you for certain, but make him work for it. Let him prove what a wonderful man he is, so you'll never doubt it."

"It's not him I doubt," Cass said without thinking. Then shaking her head, she fled, as she heard Savannah give her the blessing of a head start.

"Lucas, I need to ask you something."

CHAPTER EIGHT

*S*he had a problem, though. Where a life-changing orgasm could make her merely short of breath, her own emotions could apparently make her hyperventilate. Why did this have to happen now? She'd avoided this type of thing for so long, blown off any attempts to get below the surface. Work, making money, taking care of the kids, that was what came first.

Matt was on the top floor, so she hit several buttons in the elevator and got off on the fifteenth, fleeing to the stairwell. She went down a couple flights before she sank down on a middle step and fought for air. After spending twenty-four hours with this group, any other idiot would have removed the damn thing. Changed into a sports bra that allowed an Olympic runner freedom to drink in gallons of oxygen. It was a good lesson—the weapon that gave you an advantage in a world of mildly aggressive dogs could be turned against you in the company of a pack of sleek, sexy predators.

Her mind was a mess. She'd be hard put to outthink Nate, her youngest brother, let alone someone as sharp as Lucas. But she would try. He had a high opinion of her bravery, so if she went the coward's way, maybe she'd give him the slip. She waited, heading down to the lobby after about ten minutes, figuring he would think he'd missed her. He knew where her office was, but that was her turf. He'd have lost the strategic and tactical advantage. Maybe now was the time to take that week of vacation she'd been thinking about. Take the kids somewhere camping.

Maybe the remote mountain ranges of Tibet.

She had to be wearing his shirt, feeling its heat and scent against her flesh, every movement of the fabric like his touch. She thought seriously about stripping it off, leaving it lying on the stairs and stomping through the lobby in just the corset and skirt. But it was a fall day outside and she wasn't foolish enough to risk the cold, since she'd also left her coat behind. She'd get another.

When she reached the lobby level, she slipped off the heels and stepped out the stairwell door onto the slick tile floor. Her legs were still shaking, down to her quivering ankles. She wasn't going to risk making more of a fool of herself than she already had, but Lucas had been right. She hadn't felt decimated in their eyes. Only in her own.

And there he was, like a promise. Sitting cross-legged on the floor in his cotton T-shirt, untucked over his slacks so she couldn't help thinking about running her hands up his flat stomach beneath it. He'd shrugged the suit coat over it.

The stairwell door closed behind her as he lifted his gaze. "Why didn't you just come up the stairs to find me?" she asked.

"I figured it's like the women's restroom. That sanctuary rule you all have." When she raised a puzzled brow, he clarified. "If a lady goes somewhere by herself, you give her a few minutes. Particularly if she seems to need it. Then, there were all those stairs." He gave a mock shudder. "Exercise. I might get sweaty."

Back in the glade, his body had looked like it was oiled under the touch of the sun. She shoved the distracting image away. "Wasn't I in the restroom yesterday?"

"Sometimes a woman doesn't need sanctuary. Not that kind."

"Oh." She narrowed her eyes. "And you're a good judge of that, are you? You're insufferably irritating."

"Not arrogant?"

"Arrogant men like being told they're arrogant. Romance novels have made them think that's a good thing."

A trace of humor went through the serious gray eyes. "I owe you lunch."

"You don't owe me the meal. I pay, because you won."

"No, I didn't." Rising, he brushed off his slacks. "Because I hurt and upset you."

"So let me out of it, then."

"No. You don't need that."

"Of course I don't." She closed her eyes. When she opened them, he'd taken a step forward. Maybe two, for he was directly before her now. When he looked down at her sheer stocking-covered feet, her painted red toenails, she tightened her grip on the straps of her heels. "Your floors are terrible. I'm surprised you don't have lawsuits."

"They're pretty, though. Ben makes threatening lawsuits go away. I think he has connections to the Irish mob. Either that or he takes plaintiffs out and drinks them to death."

She stared at him. "You completely overturn my world, transform a business meeting into a...I don't even know what to call it. A chessboard to accomplish getting up my skirt, and now charm and humor are supposed to work."

He looked toward the ceiling, pondering. "Fairly good summation. At least everything except it being all about getting up your skirt. Though that was a pretty good side benefit."

When she made a sound between a snarl and a sob, he caught her arms. Unfortunately for her, fortunately for him, he hadn't forgotten the strength of her right hook. He pulled her against him, holding her there as she struggled.

"Let go."

"Cassie, listen. Stop it and listen, will you?" When he gave her a little shake, she wished she still had on her heels so she could have punctured his foot. But when she looked up in his face, she didn't see anything that suggested he was making light of the situation. Far from it.

"You've got some formidable shields, and I'm not going to apologize for using the resources I have to get past them. Because you know as well as I do that what's upset you has nothing to do with me getting up your skirt. If that was the case, you never would have stopped me a month ago. It would have been a fun fuck, and two adults would have gone their separate ways.

"But I got in. In just those few minutes. So you're scared shitless about what I'm going to find now that I'm there. Which means it matters to you." A grim smile touched his mouth, though his eyes remained hard. "Which also gives me hope that this is more to you than just getting into my pants."

She fixed her attention stonily on his chest. "I had it all planned out. I was going to use you and cast you aside."

"Like yesterday's Wall Street Journal." Lucas sighed, gathered her in, letting his chin rest on top of her head. "You know, some of those articles are good reference material."

As she let out a muffled snort, Lucas rubbed his hands up and down her back. "God, I want to get you out of this damn thing, feel your skin."

She couldn't agree more, but she drew back. "Lucas, let me put on my shoes."

"No, you're right. You'll break your neck in these."

"I'm not walking through the K&A lobby with the CFO, in nothing but bare feet."

"Okay." Letting her go, he pulled off one loafer and then the other as she watched, nonplussed. He considered his black dress socks. "We had a sliding contest down here, late one night."

"A what?"

"Sliding. You run fast and then slide in your socks across a slick floor? We had a bet on who could slide the farthest from a certain point. Kind of like skeet, with people. Then we did all sorts of crazy acrobatics. We had an audience of homeless people standing outside the window, staring at us before it was all over."

"Who won?" Cass asked, for lack of anything else to say, her mind torn between the intensity of their exchange only a breath ago, and the whimsy of seeing the K&A team play like boys at rugby in their own lobby.

"Peter. Damn mutant cyborg. He can run the fastest. I guess that's a good thing, since when people are trying to blow you up or put bullets in your ass, being fast is important."

She shook her head. "You're insane."

"We're human, Cass. That's all. We're all kids playing grown-up. We do the best we can."

Taking her hand and holding his shoes, he walked from the elevator and stairwell area into the lobby. She thought about digging in, but the floor was slick enough he'd probably haul her forward like a sled dog, so she went along with him.

Traffic flow was always steady through the K&A lobby, and today was no exception. Some of the faces were known to her, but somehow with Lucas holding her hand and moving along as if it was the most normal thing in the world to be padding across the floor in his socks, her in stocking feet, she was able to assume an almost nonchalant air.

As the receptionist gave them an amused glance, they won a snort from the security guard, who obviously knew Lucas. Then they were past, heading for the revolving door. "You're shorter this way," he commented. "Petite, like a doll."

"If you say Barbie, I'll sweep your legs and crack your skull on your pretty shiny floor."

"Ouch. Kung fu Barbie." Laughing, he dodged her shove, came back, and claimed her hand. "There's the biker chick who stole my heart." Guiding her into the revolving door, he took the same section, crowding her until they emerged into the crisp fall air that nevertheless was full of sunshine. When she started to put on her shoes, he shook his head, pulled her out of the flow of foot traffic. "Feel the warmth through the concrete."

"My stockings will tear. And the rest of me is a little cold."

"I swear, you're as bad as working with metal. A man has to fire you up to get you to bend." Gathering her against him, he wrapped her up in the slack panels of his suit coat. "Now, feel the heat through your soles. Doesn't that feel good?"

Cass resisted the urge to bury her face into his shirt, rub her cheek against his chest beneath the stretched cotton. Instead, she tipped her head back to look at his eyes, narrowed against the glare, the sun forming a halo limning his golden hair.

Yeah, right. Definitely a trick of the light, that. "Yes," she admitted, glad he didn't know what really felt so good to her. The strength of his arms, his body pressed close. The coat around her, the way she'd imagined.

"Here comes our limo, to take us to lunch." At her arch glance, he shrugged. "What's the benefit of being a big shot at K&A if you can't use the limo pool for lunch?"

"You don't have a car?"

He grinned. "You saw it in my office."

"You ride your bike to work? Where do you live? Are you insane?" She looked at the busy downtown traffic.

"It was about ten miles in New Orleans. Here it's about fifteen. It's a good way to start the day. I do have a car," he added. "I only use it when I have to. Green footprint, and all that."

"Glad to hear it. Because I'm not going on a date on handlebars or pedal pegs."

"Progress," he smiled, holding her closer, his hands low on her hips. "You're calling it a date."

Cassandra didn't want to be so comfortable in his company. She needed to be out of sorts with him, convince herself she felt used, exposed, forced to an unwelcome vulnerability. But she wasn't in the habit of lying to herself. She could avoid what she didn't want to think about, though. So for the time being she decided not to dwell on the fact he'd made her do the unthinkable. As well as left her with a frightening need for more of him.

In the limo, he slid an arm along the back of the seat, giving her a loose sense of being encircled, particularly when he toyed with her hair, coaxed her with amusing guile into leaning across him as he pointed out a landmark of interest. When she leaned back, she found his arm settled on her shoulder, holding her closer.

"I said lunch," she said. "Then you said I could walk away."

"Is that what you want to do?" he asked. "Walk away? Why won't you give this a shot, Cass?"

"I don't really have a choice, Lucas. My life has no room for something like this. Much as I might want it." She needed to give him that, but she regretted it, because the softening of his expression made her wish fiercely she had more to give him.

"There are always choices. Let's at least talk about what the obstacles might be. Let me get to know you," he insisted. "I want to know you."

"I can't—" Thank God, her cell rang, but then she saw the caller ID.

No, not right now. The timing couldn't be worse, or more ironic. She told herself to ignore it, even as she knew she couldn't. Any more than she could cover the questions it would raise.

Suppressing a desire to scream, she took the call.

"Yeah, George... How long ago? You should have called me." She bit her lip. "Yes, I know you're busy... No, I'll come get him. Yes, I will... Damn it, George, we've been through this. I can't." She shook herself. "I'll just be there in a minute, okay?"

When she disconnected, Lucas's eyes were on her face. Miserably, she averted her own, looked out the window at a world where the sun had dimmed, and everything she'd just done and enjoyed was laced with bitterness. "I'm going to have to skip lunch. If you'll stop, I'll get a taxi."

"Cass. Tell me what's going on."

Tiredness had taken over her features the moment she looked at her caller ID, and there was a pain in her eyes Lucas wanted to erase. He touched her hand, but she drew away, shook her head.

"My brother has some problems. He got picked up. Again. I need to go get him."

"This is one of the reasons you think I shouldn't get involved with you." When she pressed her lips together, he sat back, suppressing his own frustration. "Max, take us to the District One police station, will you? I assume that's where he is?"

"What?" Her gaze snapped to him. "I don't want you involved in this."

"Tough. Now tell me what we're dealing with."

"*We're* not dealing with anything," she said sharply. "I'm just going to get him. This is my business, Lucas. There's no need to involve yourself."

"No need at all, if my interest was only in your beautiful body and eager pussy." He'd pitched his voice low, but it still made her attention jerk toward the driver then back to him, her face burning.

"That's not what I meant," she hissed.

"Yeah, it was. You like men, Cass, but you view them like pets. You can only count on them for certain things, and you're wholly responsible for taking care of them. Which, for what a dog or cat provides us, is a wonderful symbiotic relationship. When you apply that to a human, it's way too much work."

"Don't you analyze me," she warned. "We're not in a board room now. I can make Max stop this limo, tell you to kiss my ass and go on my way."

"We're almost there." Lucas studied her. "I'm not trying to threaten you, Cass."

"Yes, you are," Cass retorted. She tossed circumspection out, since he already had. "Okay, we can do sex. Hell, I'd be happy to fuck our mutual brains out. You're the first man I've met in a while that might actually satisfy me without taking too much time out of my day. But my cunt is not the gateway into my life."

The limo veered, a quick brake. Lucas sent a grimly amused glance toward the front. "All right up there, Max?"

After clearing his throat, the driver, a man who looked to Cass like he also served as a bouncer, spoke. "Er, yes, Mr. Adler. I'll just, uh, raise the glass. I'd like to listen to some music."

"You can stop right here, Max, and let me out," she ordered.

Max shifted his gaze to her in the mirror, then back to the road while Lucas sat silently. "All due respect, ma'am, but we're in a section of town where I wouldn't kick my worst enemy out of the car, let alone a woman. Mr. Adler isn't going to allow it anyhow."

"I see the whole unapologetically male thing extends to your staff as well," she said through gritted teeth as the glass scrolled up with a quiet hum.

"You have more kids at home," Lucas said. "Don't you? Are they yours?"

"How did you—"

"Because I'm as good at this as you are, and that was a rotten attempt to freeze me out. Now are they yours?" Despite his indication that he was aware she was being defensive, the temper in his expression said he wasn't going to let her insult him again without consequences. Cass wasn't sure she could handle his idea of retribution right now.

"Yes. Siblings," she stated stiffly. "Five of them, from ages five to sixteen."

He blinked. "Your parents—"

"Are no longer part of the picture. Haven't been, for a long time." She shook her head, looked out the window. "Please stop, Lucas. Please. Just...stop."

Mortified, she had to fight back tears. She could already feel the weight of what she was about to do settling in the pit of her stomach.

She'd spent too much time in fucking hospitals and police stations. If he said one more word, she was going to lose it.

Instead, she stiffened as his arm settled on her shoulders. To her surprise, he didn't say anything further, just squeezed lightly, a reassurance, his hand stroking her upper arm. A soothing she'd be crazy to take. Like lying down for one minute at home when she was so tired, or taking one more bite of chocolate, things she'd taught herself not to do. But Lucas had undermined some of her normal defenses, to say the least.

"If I put my head on your shoulder for a moment, will you be quiet and not say anything?"

In answer, his hand molded itself to her temple, easing her down to his shoulder. He kept it there, just stroking her as the limo made its way through the traffic toward the police station.

George was the uniform who worked the beat where Jeremy most often was picked up. He'd known her for some time, one of the cops who'd been called to the house for domestic disturbances involving her mother, sometimes her father. So when Jeremy got picked up, he usually tried to keep him from being processed, giving her the chance to come retrieve and talk some sense into him. Occasionally, he'd suggested that shipping Jeremy over to the East Baton Rouge holding facility to cool his heels might not be a bad idea. But they'd been that route before and she wouldn't do it again, not when she had a choice.

She'd asked Lucas to head back to his office or, at the least, to stay in the car, neither of which he did. So he was a quiet, unobtrusive shadow behind her as she went through the far-too-familiar routine.

"I'll send him out front," George said, giving Lucas a quick cop assessment. "You can head him off before he takes off."

"Thanks."

He nodded, gave her a pitying look she hated, particularly with Lucas there to see it, too. Turning without another word, she headed back out, aware that Lucas held the door for her, his fingertips grazing her lower back as they left the station. She moved a few steps down the sidewalk, and took a seat on a bench. Lucas stood beside her. She wondered why he didn't sit down, then realized he was blocking her from the chill wind that was sweeping garbage along the sidewalk. He put his jacket around her, made her put her hands through the sleeves without making her talk.

That simple kindness could have broken her, but fortunately Jeremy came out the front then. He saw her immediately, of course. She always came to get him.

It was hard to comprehend everything that passed over his face. Derision, hunger, need. Waste was what she usually saw. Features too gaunt, the eyes burning or distant and vague, depending on whether or not he was still riding his latest hit. He'd inherited their father's height and good looks, as well as the addictive personality that had made her daddy a drunk. Unfortunately, the height and addictive personality were all Jeremy had left. Her twenty-four-year-old brother had the face of a man thirty years older. On the last visit, she'd heard one of the uniforms mutter to George, "She won't have to waste her time on him much longer. We'll find his body in an alley soon enough."

She couldn't argue with the truth of that either. But she couldn't give up on the brother who'd gone from recreational drugs in junior high to hardcore abuse, in order to blot out what was happening at home.

"Rescued by big sis again." He spread his arms out as she approached him, noting his calculating look toward Lucas and the limo. "Glad you could fit me in before your big date. Going to the prom?"

"You're looking worse, Jer. Why don't you let me take you somewhere, buy you some lunch?"

"Got things to do. You can give me the cash, though. I'll pick something up at the deli. Since you've got funds to spare."

She shook her head. "You'll just buy another fix. How are you buying your drugs, Jer? You know, possession is far different from dealing. You could—"

"Go to prison for a long time. So much worse than my life now."

She knew better than to engage, but then again, these brief minutes every few weeks were the only chance she got. "You chose this life. You can choose something different. Let me take you to get a sandwich. We can talk about it."

"At home?" The thread of hope behind the derision ripped her heart out of her chest, but she maintained a neutral tone.

"You're not allowed to come there. Not as long as you're strung out. It hurts Marcie and the others too much. Jessica really misses you. If you'd just let me get you into a program—"

"Been there, done that. Don't give a shit," he said bluntly. "Fuck off, sis. Don't need help from someone with a silver spoon stuck up all her holes but nothing to give her brother. Maybe that's your problem. If you'd given me more of a chance to be the man of the family, rather than taking on the role yourself, then maybe I wouldn't have turned out like this."

"I was the oldest, Jeremy. You know I—"

He cut her off with a sharp gesture. "I'm only two fucking years younger than you. But you had to run it all, do it all, make me feel even more like a screw-up."

She really did know better, but her nerves were frayed, firing her temper. "I tried that, remember? While I was trying to get my degree, you invited your creepy friends over to shoot up. You remember how one of them tried to rape Marcie when she was thirteen?" Cass stepped into him, bumping his toes. He stank. God, when was the last time he'd bathed? "Or were you too stoned to remember your sister screaming for your help?"

"Back up off me," Jeremy snarled, shoving her back, curling a hand into a fist. And found that hand caught, his body yanked around, hard gray eyes inches from his face.

"I don't care if she is your sister, you don't hit girls," Lucas said evenly. "And you sure as hell don't hit her."

"So she finally got herself a boyfriend. I was beginning to think she prefers pussy, only she's so cold you'd have to use a hairdryer to get anything up her cu—"

Lucas hauled him up onto his toes. "Finish it, and you'll be on your ass picking up your teeth. She may see her baby brother, but I see a piece of shit. You shut it, or I will shut it for you."

Cass had frozen. In her anger, she'd almost forgotten Lucas was with her, at her back. Cold, controlled, his eyes like steel. Her brother was enough of a street creature to know when the odds were against him. He shut up, though he glared.

"She weighs nothing, comes up to your chin, and you were about to hit her with a closed fist. Jesus." Lucas thrust him off, away from Cass, hard enough to send Jeremy stumbling, and she didn't miss that Lucas positioned himself between them. "If nothing else, that should tell you that you need help. You're absolutely right. She does need a man to help her lead the family. Get into rehab, stick with it. Admit you need your family's help. That's what a real man would do."

"Jeremy." Recovering, Cass stepped around Lucas. "Please, let us help."

"Fuck off." Jeremy took off at an awkward run, his limbs uncoordinated so he stumbled over a couple cracks on the pavement, but kept going.

She almost gave chase, then felt the gentle but firm restraint of Lucas's hand. Pulling away, she rubbed her forehead, counted to ten. "I'm not in the mood for lunch anymore." She didn't think she could bear to look at him, but then Lucas touched her face, surprising her such that she looked up at him.

"I'm sorry, Cass."

"No. Nothing for you to be sorry about."

"Yeah, there is." He looked down the sidewalk, where Jeremy had stopped, backpedaling when he realized they weren't following. He shot a middle finger at her, shouted something intelligible, and then turned, striding away among a largely apathetic crowd who recognized a junkie when they saw one. "That's something for everyone to be sorry about."

Moving farther from his comfort, she stared at a homeless person propped against the side wall of a storefront, sheltering from the wind. "I live in a safe, beautiful house. I have a security guard and a gate. Specifically so he can't be there."

"Has he been through rehab?"

"Twice. Ditched it both times. I had to make sure he couldn't get to the girls and Nate," she added, a steadying reminder. She wouldn't let Lucas see her fall apart over this. More than that, she wouldn't do it to herself. "They'd fall right into his traps, his sob stories. But I keep..." Her voice trembled again, despite her attempt, but she steadied it with a fierce shrug of her shoulders. "Well, that's that, then."

"No. What?" He took her by the shoulders, wouldn't let her go when she pulled. "Tell me, Cass."

"I keep telling myself not to think of him as my brother anymore. Because he really isn't, not anything like what I remember. But he is. He is." And she couldn't help it, the tears were coming, the sobs, and she couldn't stop them. "Sometimes I just want it to be over. I want to grieve him all at once, rather than these bits and pieces."

Appalled at the words she'd said, bitterness gave way to something else. *Oh, God, I can't do this here.*

At her look of total panic, Lucas simply picked her up off her feet, right there on the sidewalk in front of the police station, and strode back to the limo. Cass wanted to protest, but she couldn't. The tears were overwhelming her. This was Lucas's fault. This whole well of emotions he'd opened up in her today and yesterday, it was spilling out now, in the place she could least afford the show of weakness.

As they approached the car, she remembered he'd sent Max off to find some lunch, but her gratitude for that did little to ease the pressure inside her. When he slid her into the second seat and got in, she struck out at him, intending to castigate him for treating her like some weak-kneed female. Only somehow she ended up clutching the T-shirt instead, gripping it hard enough to rip, as she tried to pull apart something other than her own insides. He folded his arms around her, brought her against the cotton.

"Goddamn it, Cass, let it go. Anyone can tell it's gnawing at you like a cancer. I'm not going to hold it against you."

She broke. Sobbed out the frustration and misery. She couldn't remember the last time she'd cried about it, because it hurt so much to do it. His hands were between them, pulling the borrowed shirt free of her skirt, as she hiccuped painfully. Now he reached beneath it and unhooked the corset, all the way down, just one of the ways he was easing the combustible emotions pouring out of her. She didn't try to stop him, though in hindsight she doubted he would have let her this time. His hands slid in under it, replacing the stiff stays with heat, the welcome touch of his fingers, molding over her bare rib cage, becoming a different form of support as she gulped in the air she needed for the sobs.

By the time she eased up, she was sure she'd turned her makeup into a raccoon's mask, but embarrassment was getting to be a lost cause with him. Repairing the damage to her pride wasn't worth the effort.

"Sshh." Lucas was murmuring to her quietly, she realized, and had been doing so for a while. As she pushed herself up, trying to avert her face, he drew her back, wiping her eyes with the fresh handkerchief from the pocket of the coat she was still wearing.

When she tried to take it, do it herself, he let her, but he kept her within the curve of his arm, stroking her hair, his other hand settling on her hip, holding her in a secure circle. He pulled the corset out from under the shirt, away from her body, and folded it on the seat beside him, out of her reach. "You don't need this. Not with me."

Exhausted enough not to argue, she leaned into him. She shrugged out of his coat, leaving it on the seat with the corset, so her breast mashed into his hard chest in a comforting way. There was no shield between them now, on several levels. She'd just revealed far too much to him, and there was an ache inside her she was tired of feeling. His body was solid heat, and the steady drum of his heart was a counterpoint to the erratic beat of her pulse. It reminded her there was a way to assuage the loneliness and despair of all of it, at least for a few minutes. The way she'd wanted him to do from the beginning.

Surging up, she found his mouth with her own, awkwardly enough she thought she might have cut his lips with her front teeth. However, as she locked her arms around his neck and straddled him, she tossed aside control or finesse and demanded from his mouth what some deep part of her was sure only he could provide. No logic or rationality to it, those two things she'd always allowed to guide her life. She willed him to know what she wanted without words.

His hands slid under the shirt again, caressing bare skin, marked with the impressions of the tight corset. Finding them, he spoke against her mouth, a soft admonishment as he stroked abraded skin. But he also brought her closer, and the first time both breasts touched his chest, she moaned in his mouth, her hand dropping down to feel him beneath his thin shirt. Cotton felt so good when it was fitted over a man's firm, hot skin, imbued with his scent.

His arms circled her back, letting her feel the imprint of his fingers on her flesh, learning the curves of her, learning where she liked to be touched. If it was Lucas, she didn't care where, just that he touched her. She ground herself against him, against the unyielding hardness of his cock.

"Cassie," he said, his voice harsh as he wrapped his hand in her hair to hold her back a necessary inch, though his eyes were full of reassuring desire. "We're in front of a police station. We can't do this here."

"The windows are tinted. I need you to make me come. I need to come, and only you...I only want you to do it. Make me do it. Here. With you inside me. Not any other way. I want you to just fuck me, the way you've been wanting to do it." She wanted to be taken, swept away. Wanted to smell him and the vehicle upholstery, his suit, bite his irresistible mouth as he slammed her down on him.

As her long nails stabbed him through his shirt, her eyes were half-wild, like a feral cat. Lucas suspected she wanted the wildness, all the world narrowing to just that and not any of the other nightmares she was facing.

"I don't want to just fuck you, and you know it. That's not what you want either." He caught her wrists, holding her. "Cassie, look at me. I want to make love to you. Take you into my bed and keep you there a few decades, savor every inch of you. Make you scream yourself hoarse, and mark every part of you as mine. Make you want to be mine."

"No." She shook her head. "That's not what I want."

"It's what you need." He made himself soften the words, though he kept enough steel in his voice to hold her attention, mindful of whom he was dealing with. "In a few minutes, Max is going to be back. He's going to drive us to your home, and that's what we're going to do."

"I haven't agreed to that." Her expression fired, but he saw fear behind it.

"You want me enough to take it how you can get it," he said shortly. "This is the offer that's on the table. You willing to take the risk that I'm right? That it will be hell and gone from just fucking?"

She stared at him, and her big blue eyes, the need in them, almost broke his resolve. He'd take her anyway he could get her, too. Wasn't that a hell of a discovery? If another tear fell, he'd be a goner.

"You...can't. My sisters are there."

"Okay, then." Taking a deep breath, he considered that new variable, an obvious one that had been clouded by lust. "Then we go spend the afternoon with your sisters. I'll figure out an option for the evening. You keep some energy in reserve."

She nodded, her mind in obvious confusion. "Lucas, with them in the house, we can't—"

"Cassandra." He framed her face in his hands, held her captive. "I've had enough of playing games about this. You hear me? When I take you to your bed tonight, it won't be blatant or inappropriate, but I'm going to be there for breakfast. I'm going to become part of your life, and theirs. We're going to see where this takes us. You deserve something for yourself. I'm that something. What better example could they have of what sex is supposed to be about, than a guy who's head over heels about their sister? Someone who is willing to stay for breakfast?"

She shook her head, trying to pull away, escape. "Lucas, you know I have absolutely no way to process the logistics of any of this."

"I'm the bean counter, remember?" He smiled, though he wanted to bring her back to his chest, if for no other reason than her generous breasts and the aroused nipples beneath his borrowed shirt were going to make him let go of any resolve at all. He'd fuck her brains out in the backseat until the violent rocking of the car gave them away and they spent the night waiting for Ben to come make bail for them. "Let me deal with that. Don't let it be about consequences, worries, or how the world can suck and things go bad. For once, just take it." He gave her a fierce look. "Take the moment and see if it can lead to a lifetime."

"I don't know," she said uncertainly at last, so unlike herself that he wanted to hold her tight, in comfort this time. But he knew you had to close the deal before the opposition backed out. The most important thing was the signature on the bottom line, and the kiss he crushed on her lips now, bringing those delicious breasts back in contact with him, was a definite signature. With a flourish. So definite that he couldn't help crushing all of her to him, pressing the hard weight of his need between her legs, eliciting a provocative whimper from the back of her throat.

"I want to go home," she said again, gratifyingly breathless. "I need to see the rest of my family."

"Okay. One condition. You tell me about them. About you. Give me that."

When she started to shift, he adjusted her so she was no longer straddling him, but he kept her cradled in his lap. More importantly, it allowed her to stare out at the parking lot, the dismal landscape of the police station, rather than at his face, which he knew might help her talk about what was obviously difficult. But he linked his hand with hers, a simple sign of intimacy and support he hoped would help. She squeezed down on his fingers, and just when he thought he'd have to prod some more, she spoke.

"My mother was mentally ill." She gave a hopeless laugh. "The diagnosis just depended on what drug cocktail they fed her. By the time I was fifteen, I was caring for the kids. She stayed in her bed all the time. My father was okay when I was little, but then he let his alcoholism get the best of him and became a here-again, gone-again presence. Only came back long enough to get her pregnant and then take off again. Which of course would screw up her meds schedule. One of the nurses took pity on me, told me about a birth control that wouldn't adversely interact with her drugs. I got it from a clinic, saying it was for me, and put it into her food after that."

Lucas hoped Max wouldn't return too soon. It was an odd setting for it, but he found himself blessed by this quiet moment, just the two of them, her opening up to him at last, trusting him. "How did you get to Steve Pickard?"

"In high school, I was doing early college coursework for a business degree. Did an internship with him. He learned about my situation, and instead of seeing me as a liability, he groomed me. He more than took a chance on me. He saved me, and my family."

The truth of it was obvious from the emotion that crept in her voice. Lucas made a mental note to put Pickard Consulting at the top of the list of those who could ask K&A for anything.

Cass was silent a moment, remembering when Steve had cornered her in a cubicle, a defensive sixteen-year-old, and told her he was going to pay for a part-time nanny to allow her to expand her studies, go to a local college for her degree. Before she'd been able to reject it, he'd told her flatly that she was an investment. *"You're a damn teenager, raising a bunch of kids as if they were your own. I've heard you on this phone every other day, handling social workers, police, doctors, nurses, your own fucked-up parents. You've done all that, managed to keep your family together, and worked this job, balanced it with school. Anyone who has those skills has the makings of the best negotiator I can buy."*

He'd been a frequent visitor at her home ever since, particularly at holidays. He'd become a grandfatherly figure to Nate, taking him out on trips, doing guy things. Otherwise the little boy would have been raised only by females, since she'd obtained restraining orders against both his father and older brother, with George's help.

"You've denied yourself relationships to protect them."

"Yes," she snapped, defensiveness surging forward again. "That's what you do when you have kids. I have four sisters, Lucas, four very pretty sisters, not that that matters, from ages eight to sixteen."

Catching her chin, he forced her face up. "You don't think I—"

"*No.* No." She recalled herself enough to close her hand on his, realizing his comment had been an observation, not an accusation at her prolonged silence. "I know you would never. But the news is full of women who let their personal needs interfere with their first responsibility, to their children. And these girls and Nate have dealt with so much. They require a stable influence in their life, one person who puts them first."

"You're right. They do." He held her gaze. "Part of teaching kids about life is letting them see a healthy, loving relationship between two people that includes them, doesn't leave them out. But it should also teach them they don't get to be number one in every situation. Life is about give and take, sharing. Their big sister deserves a life, too, if she's busting her ass to give them everything they need."

She rubbed her forehead. "Lucas, I'm just not sure—"

"When did the corset come into it?" He glanced toward the garment, still folded on the seat, but then brought his attention back to her neckline. Because it was his shirt, he didn't need to slip a button to let his finger play along the curve of her breast in the opening, using a silken lock of her hair to tease the skin. Cassandra was mesmerized by it, the intent way he looked at her body. At her. She swallowed.

"You're trying to distract me."

"Is it working?" His eyes were even more silver in this light, she noticed, his brows a tarnished gold. No man should have a nose that straight, which now coaxed the trail of her fingertips, down to his lips, which pressed against them, a lingering kiss as she drew away, considered him.

"There were some really rough days," she relented. "Fighting with social workers, my mother's doctors, the police, when Jeremy acted up. Trying to keep my dad out of our lives. One day, I just lost it at the family services office. When I was screaming and crying, some part of me stepped outside myself, took a hard look. Not just at me, but the people around me. I realized I looked just like everyone else there. Run down by life, my behavior and my appearance resulting in a complete lack of credibility. I started paying attention to people who commanded respect, how they handled themselves and spoke, and realized it had nothing to do with money. It had to do with confidence and self-respect."

"And the corsets?" he persisted. "How did that happen?"

She colored a little. "If you laugh, I will smack you."

He forced a smile. "I won't laugh." In truth, Lucas didn't feel anything like laughing.

"The night after that happened, I couldn't sleep. I caught one of those black-and-white movies based on a Jane Austen novel. Looking at the women in corsets, I realized how constrained and elegant they had to be, and figured the outfit helped them maintain that composure. During that time period, everything had a required behavior, so they probably felt like screaming, too." Humor flickered over her soft mouth, then she glanced at the corset. "The first time I bought one secondhand, I felt silly, but when I put it on, I didn't. Controlled by that garment, I was in control of myself. People don't challenge people who approach things calmly, prepared to answer hard questions without making it personal. But you're right." Her gaze moved to his face, his strong neck, the breadth of his shoulders, feeling the controlling power of his arms around her. "It can become about something else."

She trembled a little in his arms when his expression heated at her words. "So here I am. Me and the part-time nanny, Mrs. Pitt, raised the kids. I got my degree, built my reputation in the firm, and now earn a salary that took us out of the corporate housing Steve made me accept, foiling my stubborn pride with concerns about the kids' safety, and into a seven-bedroom in the Lakeshore area."

Lucas whistled. "Pretty amazing accomplishment. Lakeshore."

"You bet your ass."

Lucas saw fire flicker in her again with the words. While he wanted to be the one to absorb her tears, give her comfort, he was glad to see the spark return. Fanning the flame, he brought her hand to his lips to tease her knuckles with his mouth, liking the way she focused on it, her mouth going soft, giving him all sorts of ideas. But he had one more difficult question. "Where is she now, your mother?"

"She died, several years ago." When she tried to draw away, he tightened his grasp and she lifted her shadowed face to his. "Got into her pills and OD'd. I blamed myself for that. I kept her at home instead of a facility because I thought that was what she needed, but we couldn't watch her the way they could have. Anyhow, I had to let it go, because I just don't have time to think about it, you know?"

And can't afford where the emotions would take her, Lucas thought.

"To be honest, I don't know if she wanted to be saved." She drew an unsteady breath. "So that's it. I come with five kids who command the lion's share of my attention, along with my work. A romantic dinner will get interrupted by a crisis involving Cheerios being super-glued into someone's hair. Sex is something you book in advance or steal five minutes in a park like a pair of teenagers, because there's little privacy at home. And I won't bring a man into their lives unless he's wanting to be part of it, not just wanting to have me."

On this her chin firmed, eyes resolute. "I may not be able to say no to the sex you're offering, but I can't take it near my siblings. They latch onto an adult male far too quickly. I'm not saying that if you walk through the door, you're agreeing to a life commitment, but you've got to care and think it's possible."

"I'm more concerned as to whether you think it's possible." He touched her face. "Because I do. I am sorry, Cass. About all of it. Especially your brother. You feel like you've failed because you can't save him yourself, but to me, it sounds like you already saved five other lives. I was right, what went through my mind that day, when I saw you in the Berkshires."

When she raised a curious brow, he drew her back to his mouth, pausing just before their lips touched. "I told myself, 'Lucas, you've just found the most amazing woman you'll ever meet. Don't let her get away.'"

CHAPTER NINE

*L*akeshore was a quiet, upscale neighborhood laid out well for children playing, people walking pets. The guard at the entrance gate possessed a steady alertness Lucas approved.

Cass's brick home likewise had a secure but welcoming feel to it, with potted plants on the front porch, a circular driveway, and a wide lawn. As they approached the house, Lucas saw a teenager on the front stoop, doing homework, while a little boy of about five years worked his way around the driveway, on a bike with training wheels.

As the limo pulled to a halt, the teenager rose, a brown-eyed girl with Cass's blond hair. Pretty enough to already be attracting men's eyes, she could use an older brother looking out for her. That was his first thought. Though something about this girl's firm chin and direct gaze, so much like her sister's, suggested she wouldn't take kindly to that idea.

When Cass exited the car, Lucas understood why she'd wanted so much to go home after the ugliness with Jeremy. She'd barely dropped to one knee before Nate had launched himself off the bike and at her, wrapping his arms around her neck. Lucas had put his coat back on her, and the child's fingers gripped the collar hard.

"Mommy!" Lucas's surprise at the address was distracted by the child's grin, competition for the brightness of sunshine. He was a younger, far less haggard version of his brother. After a brutal squeeze, he released her to gesture to the bike. "I'm riding. Marcie says I'm doing good."

"You are. I saw, coming up the driveway. Nate, Marcie, this is my friend, Mr. Adler. He works for K&A," she added to Marcie.

"You're one of the wunderkind." Marcie gave him a shrewd assessment. "The CFO."

"Your sister's mentioned me?"

"Oh, yeah. She—"

"I mentioned all of you." Cass shot Marcie a narrow glance. "Marcie is already studying business."

Marcie gave her an odd look, but then shifted her attention back to Lucas. "I looked you up. Really clever business model presentation to Harvard Business School, by the way. But where does Matt Kensington find you guys? Vegas strip shows?"

As her sister made a strangled sound, Lucas bit back a grin. "That's an HR recruiting secret," he commented gravely. "I trust you won't betray our confidence."

"Marcie." Cass sent her a quelling look. "Where's everyone else?"

"Out back. Nate just wanted to be here when you called and said you were coming home."

"Mommy, look." Nate rattled past again.

As Cass smiled at him, she murmured to Lucas, "Nate's always called me Mommy. I'm the only mom he's ever known."

Any other time, she could have managed that without the quaver in her voice, but it had been that kind of day. As she felt Marcie studying her, she cursed Lucas's intuition when he discreetly opted to fall in step with the little boy, moving out of earshot.

"It was Jeremy again, wasn't it? You have the pinched look."

Cass lifted a shoulder. "I picked him up, he's off again. Let's not talk about it, okay? Not in front of company."

"Looks like company that stuck with you through it." Marcie sent a more thoughtful look after Lucas, but then shifted to an examination of her older sister's appearance. Cass pressed her lips together under the uncomfortable appraisal, determined not to say a word to explain the man's shirt loose over her skirt. Or the suit coat she wore. A suit coat that matched Lucas's trousers. Thank God she had it, though, or the bright sunlight would have shown she wore nothing under the shirt.

Surprisingly, however, Marcie held her questions while Cass focused on Lucas.

Nate was jabbering at him. When he made a wobbling turn, Lucas steadied the seat of the bike as they continued their circuit.

"Holy God, Cass," Marcie said at last. "I saw the pictures, but I didn't think they made them that pretty without wings. Or airbrushing."

"You should see the rest of the team," Cass relented. "They're just about as bad."

"Just about? So you think he's the cutest one, then?"

"Objectively, I'd have to say so, but it's mere degrees."

Marcie tucked her tongue into her cheek. "That Ben O'Callahan looks more my type."

"He's probably about fifteen years older than you."

"So? If he was immortal, like Superman, it wouldn't matter. Ours could be a timeless love. Do you think they do internships? I could try to trap him in the mailroom or something."

"Oh, God." Cass elbowed her sister. But her tensions were easing, being here at home. Marcie could drive her crazy, but teenage silliness like this helped Cass more than her younger sister knew.

If she entertained for even a moment that Lucas could become part of her life, she knew that would mean the wunderkind would become part of it as well. Thinking of Ben around her sister almost made her laugh. She knew he'd flirt, making Marcie feel pretty and special, but fend her off appropriately, taking on a big brother role.

It made her wonder if the Knights of the Board Room nomenclature had come about because of what women's intuition detected about them. They were decent, honorable men. She'd directly experienced it when they stood around her in that tight circle, an unsettling memory under the circumstances, but she couldn't deny it had been a warm one, strangely similar to the welcome of Nate's greeting.

Unconditional acceptance.

"He's the cyclist, isn't he?" Now Jessica, her twelve-year-old sister, was on the porch, wearing knee pads. "Does he know anything about bike chains? Mine came off and something's bent, so I can't get it back on."

"How did it do that?"

"When I fell off. I was trying to turn on the ramp—"

"Where is your helmet? I told you that you're not allowed to do trick riding unless you've got it on. Marcie—"

"She had it on last time I saw her. I can't watch her every minute." Marcie fired up.

"I told you when Mrs. Pitt had to cut back her hours, you could watch them in the afternoon and I'd pay you for that. You said you could handle it." Not for the first time, Cassandra wondered why she could defuse arguments efficiently in a board room, but at home one irritation could set off a firestorm. And this was an ongoing one between her and Marcie.

"It wasn't her fault, Cass—" Jess jumped into the fray.

"Ladies. Someone mentioned something about a bike chain?" Lucas stood to their left, a steadying hand on Nate's shoulder while the little boy, his expression uncertain, looked between them.

"He knows how to fix it," Marcie said before Cassandra could head her off.

"Marcie, he's wearing a suit. He's not here to—"

"Do you wear a helmet?" Jessica asked hotly. "I've seen pictures of people your age, when they were little, and they didn't wear helmets."

"Nope, we didn't. Not way back then," Lucas confirmed. "We had bigger things to think about. Like dinosaurs and the ice age."

Jessica narrowed her eyes, undeterred. "So you didn't need them."

"No, of course not," Lucas agreed. "Overprotective, overrated—" His head jerked, a tic, twice, before he continued without blinking an eye, "Hogwash." Making a wall-eyed look, he feigned a stagger around Nate's bike. "Not a problem at all. Your sister's been kind enough to wipe the drool off my chin when I can't seem to control it. Brain damage, you know."

Jessica tried to look unimpressed, but Lucas was far too handsome and charming. In a matter of minutes, Cass saw him win the girls over. Any woman whose hormones had kicked in would be powerless against him, she knew.

"Will you fix my bike chain?" Jess asked.

"Sure," he said. "Just give me a minute to make a phone call, and I'll be right there." He glanced at Cass, moved back toward the white limo.

As she watched him, she realized he made the perfect prince on the white horse. The way he moved toward the car, the sunlight glittering across his hair. Broad shoulders and muscled arms. Cass remembered the fairy tales, and couldn't help the twinge, despite her appalled response to it. She didn't need rescuing. She'd rescued them all on her own. She wasn't insolvent, not by a long shot. She had the tuition covered for most of the kids already. Her own 401k. A home.

So why was it he made her feel rescued with just a smile, a look of those concerned eyes? God, she needed to get rid of him.

When she turned around, her sisters burst into giggles, apparently having caught her staring after him like a lovestruck moonbat. She definitely needed to get rid of him.

Instead, he stayed for the next several hours, sending the limo away. He fixed Jess's bike in no time, with only one trip needed to their well-organized tool shed. Cass sat on the back steps nearby with Marcie and let her sisters and Nate take over conversation with him. She knew she was testing him, even though she shouldn't be giving him that encouragement. But damn it and big surprise, he was good with them.

In contrast to his frank affability with the outgoing Jess and confident Marcie, as well as his more male interaction with Nate, he was quiet and patient with shy ten-year-old Talia, letting her approach at her own pace, become part of the group of girls without saying much. Next thing she knew, he was talking to her about the book she was carrying, coaxing her to tell him about it while he tuned up Jess's gears.

Then there was eight-year-old Cheryl, whom they called Cherry. She and Nate took right to him. Cass never brought men home, hadn't allowed herself a relationship where it even crossed her mind. Should she let them hope for anything? Just because she didn't allow herself hope? Damn Lucas for making her think about it like that.

When he came back at last to sit beside her, the two of them watched the kids bike around the backyard, and he asked her easy questions about them. As she responded, he leaned back, his arm braced behind her on the concrete stoop, making her want to rest against it, but she resisted, not sure if she wanted the kids to see that.

As if he'd read her mind, he nudged her arm. "Lean back." When she frowned, he tugged her hair. "You know my ride left, so you'll have to put up with me."

"You have a working thumb," she retorted sweetly. "I'm sure an amorous, lonely housewife will pick you up. You could become her afternoon fantasy."

"Sorry, already booked." The kids had reached the end of the yard and were exploring something they'd found by the fence. Before she could anticipate him, he'd captured the back of her neck and drawn her to him, holding her fast for a sweet, teasing kiss. Because the kids were distracted, it wasn't outrage that fueled her token attempt to push him away. That just resulted in her hands latching into the front of his grease-stained shirt as he deepened the kiss, making her stomach flutter and knees quiver.

When he raised his head, his eyes alone were enough to keep the fire leaping through her bloodstream. His hand was very appropriately on her waist, but the fingers hidden from view were curved over a buttock, stroking, making her want him to go lower, palm her there.

"I'm going to be your fantasy tonight, Cassie. In a few minutes, some very accomplished childcare providers will be arriving to take your kids off for the evening. Matt, Savannah, and the guys are going to take them to the movies, followed by dinner at a playhouse and arcade, and then back to Matt's place for a slumber party."

Before she could get over her shock to protest, he continued, tightening on her waist. "While they're safely being entertained, suitable to their ages, I am going to take you to your bedroom and entertain you in a manner suitable to your age. I'm going to make love to you through the night, so when there are circles under your eyes tomorrow, it will be for a better reason than working on late-night paperwork. When Matt and the team bring the kids back here, I'm going to make you sleep in and fix your kids breakfast." His eyes held her in place. "I'll bring you breakfast in bed."

"I don't know," she said at last. She swallowed. "I'm feeling overwhelmed. I'm not sure that's good, Lucas."

Spearing his fingers into her hair, he pressed the heel of his palm to her jaw. "It is good. It wasn't a no."

"It wasn't a yes." When he grinned, she scowled. "Teach me to get involved with another negotiator. Glorified bean counter."

She shook her head, pushed away from the stoop, crossing her arms under her breasts, feeling the impending evening chill. Marcie had taken the kids around to the front, and she wondered now if her sister had picked up the tone and done it with calculated intent. Having the chess pieces rearranged before she could even get a handle on the game was something she didn't like, and she didn't want him to think she'd accept being treated that way. "You know, you can't call in a babysitter every time you think there's something you'd rather be doing. That's not the way this works. I haven't had time to think this through. And tomorrow is a school day."

"Hey." As he rose, she backed up, not wanting him to touch her again. "I just wanted the first time between us to be special. Not hurried. You deserve that. And Marcie told me tomorrow is a teacher's workday. I did check on that first." He closed the distance between them in a quick step, caught her shoulders. "Cass, look at me."

At the command, she raised her angry, uncertain gaze. "I am not your drunk dad," he said. "If I'm falling for you, I'm falling for the whole package. I had a blast with the kids earlier."

"They're not always a blast."

"Really? I find that hard to believe." He gave her that little shake. "Give me some credit."

"You've only known me a day. You can't commit your whole life to this—"

"No, of course I can't. Stop it." He held her fast. "But I can say I'd like a chance. You can't deny yourself love, the possibility that I could be part of this family, for fear that I can't."

"These kids can't be jerked around anymore. I won't allow it just because you—"

"If you use the 'just because you want to fuck me' line, I will smack your ass," he said, and the steel in his gaze told her he meant it. "If that's all I wanted, I never would have come home with you. Cass, I have a sister. A divorced sister with two kids who had to live with me nearly two years when he cleaned her out of everything, the bastard. I understand the issue, and I love those kids like my own. I took over as the male role model in their life during those two years, and they still look to me that way."

"They're doomed," she said after a long moment, struggling with it.

"Don't I know it." His touch eased. "You and I have moved fast, way fast. I know that. But look at me. Look at my eyes, everything you know of me, that you know of people. Use that intuition Steve pays you so much for. If we don't work out, which I have a very good feeling is not going to be a problem, I will be as careful of the kids' feelings as I would hope to be of yours. You don't have to be so goddamned tough about everything."

She wrenched away, crunching through ankle-deep dry leaves in the yard. "Don't you get it, Lucas? It's not about that. Most women aren't tough. We're tired, we're lonely, we're afraid of failing to live up to what's expected of us. While we're looking for the one person who will accept us for ourselves and love us anyway, we're already too walled up to show him who that is. You can't let down your shields. No one can."

"You can with someone who loves you."

"Yeah, and those people come with big neon signs on them that say, 'You can trust me, I will love you through thick and thin, you can count on it.'" She backed away some more, wishing Marcie hadn't taken the kids out of earshot, wishing Lucas hadn't taken off her corset, because words were just bubbling out of her, no filter, no restraint. He was making her need to say them, standing before her, all the possibilities she wanted so much.

"There are things I've said in my head I can never say to anyone. Sometimes I'm so tired I don't want to get up ever again. Sometimes I need sex so badly I've brushed against a corner of the kitchen island and made myself come by accident, and had to cover it as a fit of coughing with the kids." She laughed bitterly. "I got the kids on track, I pay the bills, I've earned my education and reputation, and somehow I feel like all I've done with my outstanding accomplishments is build myself a great big public cage. And when that becomes too much... Ah, Christ."

She turned away, but couldn't deny his comfort when he slid his arms around her waist, held her against him, speaking into her ear. "When that becomes too much, you go to a glade in the Berkshires and give yourself twenty minutes of sanity. Everyone feels that way sometimes. But from where I'm standing, you still have a pretty damn good life, you know? You're fucking amazing, everything you've done. You're just missing someone to share it with, sweetheart. Not just to help, but to share it. We tend to make situations complex that come with big emotions, but they're usually not. Life sucks sometimes, and you need someone who can stand with you. Everyone needs that."

With a tear-streaked face, she looked up and found his gaze full of a miraculous tenderness. "I haven't cried in forever, and here it is, twice with you in one day. That can't be a good thing."

"On the contrary, I think it's a very positive sign. Hell, Cass." Turning her, he put his forehead against hers, molded his hands to her back, letting her feel the strength of his touch through his shirt. "I don't know what love is, any more than the next person. But I know when I look at you, every part of me is hoping like hell this is it. So risk it, okay? You've risked so much to get where you are, you're starting in a position of strength here." Lifting his head, he quirked a brow. "After all, I am a major catch. And I'm completely gone over you."

"And so modest." She sniffled.

"Well, first rule of negotiation, sweetheart. Start with the strongest points. Don't want to scare you off with my bug fetish or the bodies in my basement freezer."

"Bug fetish?"

"Typical woman. Her eyes go all big over the bugs, rather than my side career as a serial killer."

"How big? Are we talking spiders? Spiders are not bugs."

Laughing, he pulled her to his mouth and silenced her in a way that drove bugs out of her head.

She pulled back. "The kids."

"Gone." At her stunned look, he had the grace to look sheepish. "I'd already talked to Marcie. She took them in front when I knew the limo would be there."

"And you just assumed—"

"Yeah, I did." He looked down at her. "You know they'll be safe with us, right?"

"That's not the point. I handle my life. Their lives—"

"No question, no argument. But tonight is just for you. You won't give yourself that. I did. You and I both know you're using them as a shield."

When he closed his hands on her shoulders, bent his knees to force her to look into his face, she closed her eyes. "Lucas, I can't. I get sucked in. For so long, I wanted something like what you appear to be, so much."

You're the Holy Grail floating over the yawning Abyss. With desperation, she thought it must be the Knights of the Board Room reference making her think in King Arthur analogies. "Those kids can't afford a leap of faith. I'm what they have, and in order to be there for them, I can't risk any cracks. You're a potential earthquake."

"I think I'm flattered. But why am I an earthquake?" Somehow, while her eyes were closed, he'd backed her up against the stoop. As he posed the question in her ear, his arm circled her. Gently, so gently, with his other hand between them, he began to unbutton the shirt, teasing her skin.

"Because I need you too much. Something like you. You'll leave. You all leave. Your cocks and minds get bored."

He paused. Cass realized she'd meant to say, 'want you too much,' but they both knew a slip of the tongue like that was rarely a mistake. She couldn't take it back, couldn't cover it.

"Stop thinking. Just for five minutes, shut it off. Look at me." His expression now was one that made something flutter in her lower belly. He nodded. "Very few men would know that the avenue to your heart is, in fact, through your body, Cass. Through your submission. So the irony of it is, by taking your body exactly where it needs to go, I'm going to convince you that my heart and soul are never going to be bored with you."

She caught at the shirt as he slipped the last button. There were no close neighbors, but that wasn't why she clutched it. He put his hands over hers, began to pry her fingers away.

"I can't." Her whisper was broken. "I can't say no to you, but I can't do this."

"You're not your parents, Cass. Either one of them. You're you. And you can do it." He coaxed one set of fingers to release, then the other. Holding her wrists in one hand, he spread the two sides of the shirt open, revealing the flat line of her stomach, the crescent shapes of her breasts. "Beautiful," he murmured. "Mine. Stand still."

Turning her, he took the coat off her shoulders and then the shirt, laid them on the stoop. The skirt came next, slowly sliding over her hips, followed by the panties, so she now stood naked before him while he was still fully clothed. When she shivered, he put the coat back over her bare shoulders.

"Should we go—"

"Not yet," he said. Then he sank down before her, hands holding her hips as he studied the column of her throat, the shape of her breasts, her rib cage and abdomen. Her hips, the roundness of her buttocks, the vee of her sex, a soft pelt of hair, smooth and trim. He studied that the longest and, aside from the self-consciousness, the slight sense of embarrassment, it aroused her almost to the point of pain, the way he examined her. Her hands clutched his shoulders, then slid forward, seeking his jaw. Grasping her fingers, he sucked on them hard, strong, before pulling free, staring up at her. "Mine," he repeated. "Mine to protect. To cherish. To love. To grow old with, if we're blessed."

"Don't," she whispered. "Don't ruin it."

His eyes darkened and he bent his head, his arm curving around her to hold her in place with a hand on one hip as he brought her into him.

Cass sucked in a breath, clutched him harder as his mouth found her and he spread her stance a little wider. She had to rely on him to hold her steady, because her ground had become unstable. *Oh, God.* That mouth. Before, she'd been anchored to a chair. On her back, a table, a wall. Now the lightness of the friction as he manipulated her, let her body buck and convulse naturally, made the feeling even more maddening, a dance against his mouth. The wind moved the fall leaves, bringing her the smell of seasonal change, of grass mowed recently, of the lake.

"You're so wet for me, sweetheart," he muttered against her flesh. "Give yourself to me. Let yourself be swept away by a man's desire for you."

His tongue parted her, teased her, teeth scraping the clit as her breath rasped in her throat, her fingers digging in, the nails scraping his flesh, if he'd let her get to it. "Feel you," she gasped. "I want to feel you."

"In due time. I want you mindless first."

He thought she could think now. Catching her fingers in his hair, she pulled hard as he kept up his artistry upon her slick lips, tasting her, penetrating her, sliding over every sensitive nerve, his tongue doing flexible things a snake would envy. She wanted him.

"Want to come, with you inside me. Now."

"Not this first time," he said, without mercy. With a rake of his teeth he sent her free falling, both hands tearing at his shoulders, her bare body convulsing over him. She dug her nails into his T-shirt and the hard back muscle beneath as he held her hips fast, worked her against his mouth. His rough jaw rasped against her thighs, his fucking of her with his mouth mixed with the wet sounds of pleasure as he lapped her, took her juices into him in a way that sent powerful aftershocks ripping through her. He held on to her throughout.

When she at last tried to straighten, her body felt weak. She wasn't sure if her legs would hold, but he'd already anticipated, rising to lift her off her feet. He was still fully clothed, even down to his shoes.

"Tell me where your bedroom is, Cassandra."

CHAPTER TEN

*I*t was a quiet, dim place, the sun almost gone for the day. Through the sheer panels at her windows, he saw the shapes of the trees in the yard, while in the room there was the outline of a high tester bed, piled with pillows. A dilapidated stuffed bear was there, probably left by one of the younger children, as well as a scattering of children's books on the floor. Clothes she'd perhaps discarded this morning rested on the back of the chair. He could see the domestic scene, her trying to get ready for work, giving them all some attention before she left. There was a scattering of sticky notes on the desk and the computer screen, work waiting for her after everyone had gone to bed. A TV, some books piled up next to it. The clutter of a busy woman.

His heart too full to speak immediately, he laid her down on the mattress, that beautiful bare body that had him so primed for her it was difficult to walk.

But then, as she watched him, he collected the children's books, the work papers. He put the papers on the desk, the toys outside in the hall, setting the bear on top before shutting the door.

"This is your room, Cass," he said, turning to her. "Just the woman tonight. Do you have any wine?"

She nodded to a mini-fridge in the corner, the stand of glasses up on a shelf. "Like an evening glass of wine, do you?" he observed.

"Sometimes."

"Me, too." He went to it. As she began to shift, he half-turned. "No. Stay there."

"I feel uncomfortable, naked like this when you're not."

"This is the way I want you. Would it be easier if I tied your arms and legs, fed you the wine from my own lips? Blindfolded you, so all your senses are focused only on your body? What I do to it?"

She pressed her lips together. "I want to see you. I want to touch you."

Moving to her player, he turned on music. A smile curved his lips as Foreigner's "Waiting for a Girl Like You" came on. "I'll tie you another time, then," he responded. "But right now, you'll lie back on your pillows, high enough that your back is arched, your breasts tilted up. I want your legs spread so that I can see how wet your lips are. If I've a mind to feast on them again, they'll be ready for me."

He waited, still, his gray eyes holding hers in the soft light, the slope of his jaw made dark and sensuous in the shadows. He hadn't said "pretend" this time. Hadn't given her that out. From the look on his face, she knew he'd meant what he said. No more games. No more denying what she desired, the dark way she desired it.

She found herself sliding up the pillows and leaning back so she was in the position he'd ordered, her breasts in such wanton display she almost blushed. For all her experience in business, her knowledge of what went on in the bedroom, her couplings had been perfunctory, an exercise in mutual needs being satisfied. She'd never had a forceful or demanding lover, let alone a Dominant who could make her want to please him like this, to raise the potential threshold for herself. Seeing the look in Lucas's eyes, just a little dangerous, telling her he might not brook a refusal, brought a delicious thrill. It also made her a little embarrassed to open her legs, but when she did it, the fierce desire leaping in his eyes was reward for her bravery.

"You're dripping for me again. I'll have to come take care of that."

"Please," she whispered.

He set aside the wine, and glory be, he carelessly pulled off the T-shirt. He wore the silver medallion he'd had on that day at the glade, so as he put one knee on the bed and leaned over her, she reached up. He stilled, letting her fingers close around it.

"It has an inscription." She studied the engraving, a cross, the burst of sunlight behind it. "'The right hand of God.'"

"Savannah gave each of us a wedding gift, a groomsman gift, if you will."

A smile touched her lips. "I wouldn't have expected her to have a wicked sense of humor."

"Oh, yeah. She's just reserved at first." His voice gentled. "She never really got to love anyone, until Matt. And us."

Cass raised her gaze to his face. "So you all love her."

"Entirely. She's family. And no"—his fingers threaded through her blond hair, bringing it forward across her mouth, a whimsical gesture —"you're not a surrogate for my best friend's wife. I just happen to have a thing for good-looking blondes. But I'm partial to the ones who ride Harleys and have rapier-sharp business sense. Savannah doesn't have a motorcycle."

"But you wear the necklace she gave you, under your clothes."

Nodding, he closed his hand over hers on it, where her thumb was stroking the metal, and his flesh beneath it. "She had it blessed. She worries about me, biking in traffic. It makes her feel better, knowing I have it on. I tell her she's going to have to fire the priest if I do get run down. She says that'll just prove God knew I was too much of an idiot to waste the effort. I like wearing it. It reminds me of my connection to them. They're as much my family as the one that raised me. I was adopted, but that doesn't change a thing about who you consider your family. It's why Nate calls you Mom, right?"

Another thing he understood about her. Taking her hand, he pressed his lips to her knuckles and eased down on her, still wearing the slacks. However, she wasn't ready to complain, as for the first time the bliss of his bare chest came down against hers, the coolness of that metal. Reaching up suddenly, she gripped his neck, pressed her lips there, tasted the metal chain and heat of him as she'd wanted to do that first time.

She slid her arms behind his back, holding him as she licked and kissed his muscled skin. As she pressed her palms against the hard lines at his waist, the rise of his buttocks, his slacks bunched under the grip of her fingertips. She was so hungry for him. The need just surged up in her, as if by lying between her legs, against the core of her, his heart to her heart, he'd cracked something open so wide inside her that only tearing into him would help alleviate it.

The music selection had changed to "How to Save A Life" by The Fray, a song too poignant, too close to the way her heart felt.

As he caught her hands, lifted away from her, and used that hold to keep her to the pillows, she tried to follow him. "Lucas, I need you now. Inside me. Please. I feel like I'm breaking. I want you to do everything you said, but for this second, please."

"Okay," he said softly. He rose from the bed, finally removed his slacks and the snug dark cotton shorts beneath them.

She'd seen him with the bike shorts, which had made him all but naked, but now, to see the slim line of hips, the erect cock, rising high and hard, moisture collected at the tip, the lines of his thighs, he was—

"Beautiful," she said softly, and meant it.

His mouth tightened with emotion and he came back to her, taking her hands. "That's you, Cassandra. The most beautiful thing I've ever seen. Do I need to wear anything?"

"I want to say no, but..." She shook her head. "No one's been in my bed a long time, or been this close. Actually no one's ever been this close...emotionally. I'm sorry."

Picking up his slacks, he took care of it and came back to her, settling between her legs, looking down at her, his lips a sensuous curve. "You don't have to say you're sorry for not being with other men. I don't want anything between us either, but we can come up with something that makes that possible another day." His gaze sparked. "In the meantime, this is a prototype from one of our acquisitions, supposed to be the thinnest yet. The strongest and safest ever. You can do a product evaluation for us." When his broad head nudged her, she let out a shaky breath, aching for him, wanting him, but paralyzed by the weight of her own need.

"Okay," she agreed, but when Lucas saw a glistening at the corner of her eye, the gentle humor intended to ease her tension fled. Bending, he pressed his lips to the tear and laid his weight back upon her body. So many willing curves and fine limbs, the silk of her hair. His cock leaped eagerly, but he knew the advantage of anticipating. Plus, he wanted more than anything to eradicate the tears, even willing to set aside his own lust forever if he could keep just one from marring her perfect cheek.

Yeah, he was a goner. No doubt about it. "What's the matter, sweetheart?"

"I want you so much, but I'm afraid." Cass looked away. "People change, Lucas. You think you'll always have them, always love them, and then they change. Every time you open your heart, it happens. And this time, I'm not risking just my heart."

Hadn't she learned a long time ago that a family member could turn into someone who wouldn't love her? Or become the type of person she couldn't love anymore?

"You never want to lose control. You never want to have the unexpected happen to you. Cass." He tightened his grip until he was sure he had her attention. "I swear to you, on everything that I am, everything that I value, I will not fail you. I'm here, feel me." He pressed against her, effectively riveting her. "I'm not going to stop there. I want to be all the way in you. In your heart and soul, so you never doubt me."

"I want you so much I feel like I'm going to break. And I can't believe I'm saying these things to you."

"I know." As she buried her face in his chest, gripping him, obviously not wanting him to see her face, Lucas realized the best negotiators knew when it was past time for talk.

Pressing his lips to the top of her head, he kept his arms wrapped around her back and thrust home, deep. The tightness of her channel underscored the truth she'd told him. It had been a while, and he was fiercely glad for it. She stretched for him, her hips tilting up, her mouth open in a cry against his chest, her teeth scraping his flesh as he plunged, hard. Her legs wrapped around his back, gorgeous flexible thing that she was, and he rammed into her again, going with a more aggressive attack because he knew that was what she needed.

Every defense she'd thrown up, the fortress she'd built, she needed them shattered, because she had to be absolutely sure she could trust him, not only to reach her, but to stand with her. Protect her, love her. She needed a guarantee, even though he knew she was smart enough to realize there wasn't one. She was just enough of a woman to always hope there might be one. He could almost feel her desperation in this dark room, as her heart warred with her mind.

It was time to drive her mind out of the equation, because sometimes the heart needed to make the decision. Lifting his upper body, he drew her away from him so she was lying back on the pillows again, those delectable breasts just there for the tasting. He went to work on them, pleased to erase the unique lingering mint smell of Peter's mouth with his own, taking a nipple into his mouth, sucking as she contracted on him, her fingers raking his back.

One hand found his buttocks, exploring, pleasing herself with the feel of him. As he lashed the nipple, kneading the breast with his hand to roll the peak in his mouth, her fingers dug in. He surged into her harder, thrusting deep. He wanted her sore, sated. Her body was trembling, flushed, and he worked his tongue in between her breasts, holding the generous curves together so he was emulating the penetration of his cock. While she writhed against him, he kept his hips moving, the slow pump, deep in, slow drag out, feeling her getting wetter and wetter.

"Lucas. Come with me. I need to know you'll...go with me."

He could have exploded without a thought. He nodded.

Cass kept her gaze on his face, the gray eyes, the implacable mouth, the concentration and fire. She couldn't think, her body spasming already, but then she gave a cry of protest as he slid out of her, went down her body and suckled himself on her cunt, lifting her hips and legs so she was yanked half off the bed, clutching the head board as he plundered her, clever enough not to touch her clit and send her right over.

He'd slowed, taking his time now, and she was mewling, any type of self-control or dignity abandoned as she pleaded for what she wanted.

What was he doing? Why wouldn't he just let her go? As he turned his movements into slow licks that took her just to the edge of orgasm, held her there, she whimpered helplessly. He balanced her there with a precision that suggested he knew things about her body that she didn't. The pleading was lost as she accepted it, knew she was all his. Her hands gripping the headboard as if truly bound there said it clearly.

Whatever he wanted to do to her, wherever he wanted to take her. Somewhere in the haze of her mind, she knew that was the lesson. Give it all to him, trust him, no control of her own.

He slid down the bed, his hands caressing her legs, and came back up with the belt from his slacks. As if reading her mind, her desires, he bound her wrists, then looped and knotted the belt to the rail. "You'll get very familiar with my belt," he observed in a husky whisper, working his way back down her throat. She turned her face to his temple, pressed frantic kisses there, tried to bite at his flesh. "It will hold you like this. Or I'll use it to slap your pretty butt when you don't trust me. Make you have trouble sitting down in your meetings." He stopped over a nipple, gave it a hard nip as she cried out, another wordless plea. "You'll bite down on it when I find you for lunch, take you somewhere semi-private and fuck you up against the wall."

"Lucas, don't do this."

"Don't do what? Back you down, until you know you belong to me, every inch, inside and out? Know that you can trust me with anything, because I consider you mine to protect, look out for? Love? You, and everything that belongs to you."

"Antiquated." She muddled up the word, her tongue not working. "Ideas of male chivalry...chauvinism. Don't need you to take care of me."

"Everyone needs someone to take care of them. Now, hush. Believe in me." Lifting his head, he gave her a long look, studied her hungry face, his own taut with desire. "Search your heart, Cass. Is there even one thing in your heart that can help you make that leap? Just one?"

The taste, heavy weight, and steel of him were sending her into bliss as he braced himself over her, his muscles tightening up and down his upper body in delicious display.

With the belt and his words—hell, the past thirty-six hours—he'd pushed her past something in herself, the wall she'd built, right into something that felt more natural and true, a new garden that might just be hers to explore. She sought something there to answer his question. Because he had pushed her that far, she wasn't surprised to find what he demanded, just waiting for her recall.

It was a news clipping she'd found during her research. Matt's team had been an active part of the rescue and relief efforts during Katrina. The picture showed Lucas sitting on the tail gate of a supply truck. He'd been filthy dirty, with a group of children sitting with him. Exhausted, he'd been leaning against the side of the trailer, fast asleep. The children, a couple of them, played in the mud near him, but two or three were piled on him, sleeping as well.

She knew children. They might take toys or candy from a kind stranger, come back to him for more of the same, but in the same phenomenon seen around police stations and soldiers, children followed and stayed close to those who made them feel safe.

No matter what happened between them, Lucas would take care with her children.

And that would give her the sense of surety she needed to be his. To open her heart to falling in love with him, though she was likely most of the way there. He was right. It really didn't have anything to do with time. The deal closed early. Time just allowed all the details to be worked out.

"Lucas, please. I want you."

God, he was everything he wanted. She wasn't looking at his body anymore, but at those serious gray eyes. It made her mouth dry with need in disproportionate response to the soaking wetness between her legs. As he waited, she managed the next step. "I need you. I accept you."

The ability to tease him with her opening, the arch of her body for his hard cock, made her tremble. He seated himself in her opening, held her down when she tried to pull him in.

"One more, Cass. You owe me one more before I take you. Look me in the eyes and say it, so we both know there's no going back."

She shut her eyes, wanting to believe so much, wanting not to be afraid, knowing there was no way to do this without being afraid.

"You promised breakfast, right?"

"Chocolate chip pancakes, all the way around. Cassandra, say it."

She opened her eyes, stared up at him. "I'm yours."

Something flickered in his gaze and he slowly, slowly pushed in, going deep into her slickness again.

"I'm yours, too," he said softly. "Come for me, Cass."

"You, too," she breathed, just before her body began to buck, from no more than an artful flex of his hips, a tiny rub against her, inside and out. The feel of him, pushing in where nothing had been for a long time, was like a small, rippling, searing orgasm all its own. It built like a wave as he continued the movements, building higher as she clawed the belt binding her wrists, knowing her voice was going to be hoarse from screaming, because she was already crying out, and she wasn't even there yet.

Then he started really moving, and fire became conflagration, sweeping through her, taking her up higher, higher as he thrust home, all brutal strength now, taking her in every sense of the word. She exploded, years of catharsis contained in one blinding emotional and physical outpouring that swept her away so she could only hold him with her legs and hope he held on to her. She screamed, pleaded with him. When he released, she wished she could feel the hot stream of him filling her. But the feel of that cock, rippling with release against the walls of her channel, his harsh grunts, the brutal clutch of his fingers on her hips that would leave treasured bruises, would be enough for this moment. Until the next one.

Plaster had to be knocked out of the wall behind the headboard, but she'd figure out some way to explain that to Marcie. Maybe to Jessica. Marcie wouldn't be duped.

When she cracked open an eye at long last, the full weight of his body was on hers, his temple against hers as well. Being tied like this. Oh God, it still felt arousing, even with her body shuddering in aftermath. Who knew? He reached up, loosened the tie of the belt to the headboard, but left her wrists bound to bring them over his head, her fingers curved against the back of his neck. When he shifted and turned her to hold her in his arms, she smiled. "You're not letting me go?"

"Nope." He had his eyes closed, one hand on her ass in a possessive hold, the other around her back, his hand playing with her hair in the small of it, making her shiver.

"Why?"

"Because as soon as I get past this postcoital coma I'm in, I'm going to start all over again. I'm going to do this to you, over and over, so when the kids come back in the morning, you won't have any doubts about the fact I'm not going anywhere."

"I don't have any doubts now."

He opened his eyes, tilted his face down, filled with surprise. "You convinced me," she admitted. "You did what a great negotiator is supposed to do. I know the world's not a certain place, Lucas, but I'm going to put my faith in you. Whatever happens between us, I'll know it was worth the leap. So will you untie me now?"

His face was a study of emotions that touched her heart. Then a light smile lifted his mouth. "Soon. I promised you a glass of wine."

His gaze traveled down her body. "I never said where I was going to pour it, or the type of vessel I was going to drink from. And I find I have quite a thirst."

"You can't possibly."

"No. Men are limited in that way. But women aren't." His eyes flashing with promise, he rose, sliding her hands from around his neck to go retrieve the bottle of wine, as well as a towel from her bathroom.

As he came back, she was still halfheartedly protesting, though the shiver in her limbs and his intent gaze on her bound body told her it would do little good.

"Would you deny me, Cassandra?" He gave her the look that made her pulse leap and told her she was his, body, heart, and soul. No, she wouldn't deny him. Though next time that male propensity for post-coital coma kicked in, she was going to pounce on him, bind his hands with his belt, and go to work on every inch of his body with her mouth the way she craved to do.

"Can you do crepes? Talia loves crepes."

He nodded. "I can do things you can't even imagine. Will you deny me, Cass?"

She swallowed, all desire to tease fleeing before that expression. "No."

"Good." He put the towel down, parting her legs with a gentle but inexorable hand upon one. "Because I intend to give you everything."

He did eventually release her hands. And, as he held himself on his arms over her, in the small hours of the night, prepared to make love to her the third or fourth time—or maybe it was the fifth—she allowed herself the pleasure of finally fingering the soft hair across his forehead. Was there such a thing as a fantasy that turned into something better in reality? Could she let herself believe what had started over a month ago could be something real that lasted? Could Sleeping Beauty really be roused from her sleep by one kiss, and want to spend her life with the prince? And him with her?

She'd never given herself the luxury of hope in such a thing, with its unacceptable and often disappointing truth. But perhaps Sleeping Beauty had seen in her prince's eyes what she saw in Lucas's now as he slowly entered her once again, keeping his gaze locked on hers as her lips parted, tender body arching to accept him again. Something that wasn't disappointing, something she knew was worth working for, getting up off the princess's dais and following him into a whole new world of possibilities.

When Lucas bent, bringing his mouth to hers in a kiss that still melted her, that she suspected always would, she met it. Lifting her head, putting her hands on either side of his neck, she dug into the silk short hair at his nape, finding the rough line of his jaw under her thumbs, feeling his hard body stretched all along her softer one. She gave way before truth again and gloried in it. *His.*

"I'm going to lose that bet," he muttered against her lips.

"What bet?"

He shook his head, taking her head back to the pillow, his forehead resting on it. "Tighten on me, sweetheart. The bet doesn't matter. You're what matters. Tell me again you're mine."

She smiled and kissed him, but didn't answer. Taking Savannah's words to heart, especially in their current position, she decided she wanted him to work for it. All night, and then some.

And then she'd ask for those bracelets back.

* * *

WANT MORE KNIGHTS OF THE BOARD ROOM?
Peter Winston is K&A's operations manager and a National Guard captain. The night before he heads out on his second Afghanistan tour, he meets Dana, an Army sergeant and sexual submissive who gets into his head and heart the way no woman ever has.

Yet when they reunite one year later, life has drastically changed for Dana. With the sensual talents of the other K&A men, Peter sets the stage for another special night for them, knowing that only a submissive's willingness to trust her Master will bring her back to love and life again.

**CLICK HERE TO READ NOW
HONOR BOUND**

Reading this in print format?
Look for it at your favorite book vendor!

ABOUT THE AUTHOR

Having penned over fifty acclaimed BDSM contemporary and paranormal titles, which includes six award-winning series, *Joey W. Hill* has been awarded the RT Book Reviews Career Achievement Award for Erotic Romance. A submissive herself, Hill brings authenticity to her intensely emotional love stories.

She is grateful for the support of a wonderful and enthusiastic readership, which allows her to live on her beloved Carolina coast with her even more beloved husband and menagerie of animals.

- On the Web: https://storywitch.com
- Twitter: https://twitter.com/JoeyWHill
- Facebook: https://facebook.com/JoeyWHillAuthor
- Facebook Fan Forum: https://facebook.com/groups/ JWHMembersOnly
- MeWe: https://mewe.com/i/joeywhill
- GoodReads: https://www.goodreads.com/author/show/ 103359.Joey_W_Hill
- BookBub: https://bookbub.com/authors/joey-w-hill
- Amazon: https://amazon.com/Joey-W-Hill/e/B001JSCIW0

ABOUT THE AUTHOR

Having penned over fifty acclaimed BDSM contemporary and paranormal titles, which includes six award-winning series, *Joey W. Hill* has been awarded the RT Book Reviews Career Achievement Award for Erotic Romance. A submissive herself, Hill brings authenticity to her intensely emotional love stories.

She is grateful for the support of a wonderful and enthusiastic readership, which allows her to live on her beloved Carolina coast with her even more beloved husband and menagerie of animals.

- On the Web: https://storywitch.com
- Twitter: https://twitter.com/JoeyWHill
- Facebook: https://facebook.com/JoeyWHillAuthor
- Facebook Fan Forum: https://facebook.com/groups/ JWHMembersOnly
- MeWe: https://mewe.com/i/joeywhill
- GoodReads: https://www.goodreads.com/author/show/ 103359.Joey_W_Hill
- BookBub: https://bookbub.com/authors/joey-w-hill
- Amazon: https://amazon.com/Joey-W-Hill/e/B001JSCIW0

ALSO BY JOEY W. HILL

Arcane Shot Series

Arcane Shot

Arcane Madame

Arcane Chaos

Arcane Knight

Daughters of Arianne Series

A Mermaid's Kiss

A Witch's Beauty

A Mermaid's Ransom

Knights of the Board Room Series

Board Resolution

Controlled Response

Honor Bound

Afterlife

Hostile Takeover

Willing Sacrifice

Soul Rest

Knight Nostalgia *(Anthology)*

Mistresses of the Board Room Series

At Her Command

At Her Service

At Her Call

At Her Pleasure

Nature of Desire Series

Holding the Cards

Natural Law

Ice Queen

Mirror of My Soul

Mistress of Redemption

Rough Canvas

Branded Sanctuary

Divine Solace

Worth The Wait

Truly Helpless

In His Arms

Ignition Sequence

Naughty Bits Series

Naughty Bits

Naughty Wishes

Vampire Queen Series

Vampire Queen's Servant

Mark of the Vampire Queen

Vampire's Claim

Beloved Vampire

Vampire Mistress *(VQS: Club Atlantis)*

Vampire Trinity *(VQS: Club Atlantis)*

Vampire Instinct

Bound by the Vampire Queen

Taken by a Vampire

The Scientific Method

Nightfall

Elusive Hero

Night's Templar

Vampire's Soul

Vampire's Embrace

Vampire Master *(VQS: Club Atlantis)*

Vampire Guardian *(VQS: Club Atlantis)*

Vampire's Choice

Non-Series Titles

Chance of a Lifetime

Choice of Masters

If Wishes Were Horses

Medusa's Heart

Make Her Dreams Come True

Snow Angel (short story)

Submissive Angel

Threads of Faith

Unrestrained

Virtual Reality

www.ingramcontent.com/pod-product-compliance
Lightning Source LLC
Chambersburg PA
CBHW051246170626
46809CB00004B/1523